Runni

Leadville

Life, Love, Loss, and a 100-Mile Ultra
Marathon Through the Colorado Rockies

Brian Burk

i

To my wife,
  You treat me better than I need to be
treated. Thank you for always being there
for me.

  I Love You...More

Brian

"Life is a marathon, so let's train for it."

www.brucevanhorn.com

"I've come to face reality, I may not have the drive, genetics or time to be in a position to ever place first in my age group or ever win an event. But I CAN DO EPIC. I will do epic and I will live an EPIC LIFE."

www.briansrunningadventures.com

Table of Contents

To all the countless runners out there who have inspired me, to all the people who have believed in me, invested in me, and to my family who **LOVE** me,

Thank You

CHAPTER 1

Crossed Paths

Overhead, Brian heard the deep, vibrating and repetitive sounds that he knew to be that of the beating blades of a helicopter. The crisp air was shattered by the droning sounds of the rotary blades ripping thru the atmosphere as they propelled the helicopter towards him. He had no idea who called for help; numerous people had stopped to offer assistance. He was simply relieved that some form of assistance had arrived. Holding Abby's battered and limp body in his arms, he desperately tried to comfort her. She came in and out of consciousness as they waited for aid. He felt helpless, he only wanted to turn back time and change the terrible course of events that had played out along the side of that lonely road on an otherwise picture perfect morning.

Her eyes opened, she seemed confused until her line of sight found Brian's face. Abby took a breath. It was weak and shallow. "Brian, what happened?" she asked. Her voice was barely audible over the chaotic and muddled sounds surrounding them.

1

It took every ounce of willpower and resolve for Brian to keep his emotions together. The last thing he wanted her to see was any signs of shock or an expression of his grave concern. "Abby, I love you" He took a deep breath, "I'm so sorry. We were running and something came up from behind us." He paused to gain some strength. "It was a truck, Abby. A truck came up from behind and it hit you. You're going to be okay." He paused for a moment, then repeated himself. "Abby, you're going to be okay." Conflicted and confused, was he lying to her or to himself? Inside he cried out "Abby, you have to be okay."

Suddenly the air pressure around them changed. Dirt and debris was tossed into the air as the red and white stripped helicopter with bold letters "RESCUE" and its N-number emblazed on its side approached the ground. Brian could feel the turbulence around him pick up as the emergency helicopter landed in a nearby field. Loose grass and dirt from the roadside was flying everywhere, acting in second nature he leaned forward and held Abby tight. His body shielded her face from the flying bits of dust, rock, and dirt.

When things calmed down he looked up and noticed the rescue crews in their white and blue flight suits were running his way. Arriving at her side, they immediately went to work assessing Abby's vital signs. They asked Brian questions about what had happened and what her condition had been prior to their arrival. He was struggling to answer. In the midst of all the commotion, it was challenging to take in everything that was going on around him. One moment he had been enjoying a wonderful morning run with the love of his life, then the next second he was in the center of a cyclone of activity. His mind was numb. All he could think about was Abby. His thoughts went to the worst possible place. Was he losing her?

He tried to inform them what had happened but what came out was a jumbled mess. "We were running. There was a truck. Her head hit the ground, hard. It hit hard. Please help her." The paramedic was on the radio conferring with the medical staff at a nearby hospital. The exchange of information was rapid fire. Brian could not understand everything that was being communicated. Her pulse weak, eyes unresponsive, Abby had slipped into unconsciousness again.

"Okay, we will try to stabilize her and transport," relayed the on-scene paramedic back to the ground crew. As much as he wanted to help, Brian could only stand back and watch. He wanted to do more. He wanted to hold her hand. With every fiber of his being, he wanted to talk with her again. He wanted to tell her he loved her and he wanted to marry her. But he knew her best chance at surviving this terrible day was for him to stay out of the way. Brian had to let the professionals go to work. It was Abby's only hope.

Within minutes they had her strapped to a back board. Two men lifted her up and carried her across the road. The female paramedic followed near Abby's head and shoulders carrying a handheld monitor. Brian assumed the monitor kept tabs on all of Abby's vital signs, her signs of life. The entire movement went off like a well-rehearsed drill. This time it was for real, both for the medical team and for Abby. Brian put on a brave front on the outside but inside he was an emotional wreck barely able to keep himself together. He kept pace with all the movements, following along as close as he could. He did not want to be far from the girl he wanted to spend the rest of his life with.

Midway to the helicopter Abby eyes opened and she spoke. "Where is Brian, is he okay? I want to see him." Then she gasped out in pain.

The female paramedic comforted her, "Hun you're okay." She motioned for Brian to come forward. "My name is Judy. We are transporting you to the hospital. "Hang in there with us, okay?"

Seeing Abby come back to this world Brian quickly approached. "Honey, oh Abby, you're okay. We're taking you to the hospital. You're going to be okay. Just try to hang on. Please hang on. I'm okay. I love you...I want to marry you."

Those four words hung in the air. Time stopped and hearts raced the three members of the rescue crew looked at each other for a brief moment. Then they went right back to work.

Abby's eyes found Brian's. The two of them shared a moment in the

3

middle of all the chaos. If only for a brief second, it was just the two of them. As they approached the door of the helicopter, Abby drifted off. Alarmed Brian cried out, "Is she okay?"

"Yes, vitals are weak but the same. She's still with us, she is still fighting." "Okay guys," Judy called out "let's load her up and get moving. Time is important here."

Helplessly Brian stood by as they fastened the stretcher down inside the state of the art rescue helicopter. Not sure what to do next, Brian simply stood there. The rotor blades overhead began to speed up and the sound of the jet engines became deafening. The crew jumped into position. The paramedic took her station to the side of Abby's head. Brian stood there looking in the side door. The crew motioned for him to get in. He only needed to see the signal once. Brian instantly jumped inside, Judy pointed to an empty crew station at Abby's feet. He wanted to be closer. Brian wanted to comfort her, but he knew in his heart that she needed the skills of the professionals. Brian buckled his seat belt, leaned forward, closed his eyes and prayed.

The doors slid closed and the noise of the jet engine faded just a bit. Brian could tell the helicopter blades were increasing in speed. He held tight to the seat and opened his eyes. Abby was still unconscious. He could feel the helicopter lift off from the ground. In just a few seconds they went from being stationary in the middle of a farmer's field to reaching take-off speed and breaking the hold of gravity. Brian took a second to look outside. The scene below looked like one out of a big screen disaster movie. People were clustered together. A truck was on its side in a ditch along the road. Emergency vehicles were scattered everywhere. Brian could hardly grasp that he was caught up right in the middle of this terrible scene.

For a second he wondered about the condition of the driver of the vehicle. He never gave them a thought once he realized Abby had been hit. Viewing this scene for the first time from an outside perspective, he was now gripped with guilt. "Oh, dear God, I'm sorry I did not check on the other person, I pray they are okay as well."

Brian looked over at Judy. He reasoned that if he could see into her eyes if he could make a connection with her, he would get some indication of Abby's condition. He held fast to the hope of the best outcome for Abby. Judy was busy tending to the IVs that were running into Abby's arms. The rest of her body was covered in a white blanket with pale blue trim that stopped just below her neck. Brian had a clear line of sight to see Abby's face. Her hair was tossed around but still tied back in a ponytail. She appeared pale. He noticed a hint of bruising that began to show and there was some swelling. All Brian could think about was how he only wanted to see her smile once more, to hear her laugh and to feel the touch of her hand during a long walk. With nothing to do but to sit there during the ride to the hospital, Brian began to wonder how this was going to work out. Then as if the weight of the world came crashing down on him, it hit him. He needed to inform Abby's parents.

Brian Remembered he had his cell phone in his running vest pocket, He quickly took the phone out and waved his arms hoping to catch Judy's attention. It did not take long for her to notice his frantic waving. She looked his way. Brian yelled out so that he could be heard over the roar of the jet engines, "Parents," as he pointed back to his cell phone. She nodded her head, yes.

Frantically Brian hit his contact list then scanned the names until he found Abby's parents' number. Next to the number was an icon, it was a picture of Abby and her parents, they were all smiling. He dreaded making this call but knew it had to be done. His finger moved over the screen. He tapped the icon that would make his phone dial her parent's number. Brian's heart sank. In that very moment, he was completely lost for words.

On the other end of the digital connection, the phone rang once. Brian began to wonder, "What do I say?" The phone on the other end rang twice. "Oh, please be home." Just days ago he was considering how he would ask Abby's father for her hand in marriage and now he was trying to figure out how to explain to this man that his daughter had been hurt in a car accident.

5

On the third ring, the phone was answered. Brian instantly recognized the voice on the other end as that of Abby's father, Al.

"Hello, it's Brian"

Al had a hard time hearing him over the noise and vibrations of the helicopter.

"Brian is that you? What is going on? I can barely hear you."

"Al. Please just listen. Abby's hurt. It's bad. Please get to the ER, the emergency room at Hamot hospital now. I'm with her in the helicopter." "Please", he pleaded. "Al, get there now please!"

The only thing Brian could understand was the sound of her father replying, "Oh, Dear God, Yes, moving, we are on our way." Then the connection went silent.

Brian closed his cell phone and looked up at the ceiling of the cabin inside the helicopter. He wondered where all this was going and how it was going to end. Somehow he reasoned with himself that, it must be a dream. He closed his eyes, hoping to just wake up and be back in bed. But it did not happen that way. He was there and this was very real. The sound from the helicopters engines began to die down. Their forward motion slowed and he could sense that they were decreasing in altitude. Brian glanced out the window. This time he could tell they were close to the hospital. Within a few more seconds the helicopter was positioned right over the helipad and was descending for a perfect landing. Brian could only wonder if they had made it in time.

The doors flew open and just as fast as they had put Abby inside, they had her outside of the helicopter. The medical staff was rushing to meet her and the Medevac team. Brian rapidly unclipped his seat belt, exited the helicopter and raced after them. He was trying to stay as close as he could without hindering their efforts to provide Abby with the care she desperately needed. Within seconds the team transitioned from the helipad to inside the aerial recovery portion of the ER. Doctors came quickly from nearly every direction, each assessing her injuries. Outwardly she appeared just a little tousled if it were not for the puffiness around her eyes. Brian remembered the sound of her head hitting the roadway. The swelling of her head was now more apparent. Brian knew that's where most of the real complications would be.

In the middle of all the confusion and noise, Abby strained to open her eyes. Gathering all of her strength, she spoke. "Brian, please where are you? Please, oh please, come here."

Pushing one doctor to the side, Brian rushed forward, "I'm here, Abby. I'm here." He reached out for her hand. The coolness of her touch caught him off-guard. Fear ripped through his entire body. "Abby, I'm here," he said, his voice breaking. "I have you, honey. I'm not leaving."

Abby rolled her head in the direction of his voice, just enough for their eyes to make contact. She smiled ever so slightly when she saw him. "Brian," she paused taking a deep breath. "I love you."

The Abby closed her eyes and in that second, it was all over. Brian did not let go of her hand until the doctors pushed him away as they tried to resuscitate her. Somehow on the inside, Brian knew that Abby was gone. He stood watching as they tried to save her but knowing too well that it was too late.

The team worked desperately to save her life. During the battle for her life, they attempted to get her heart going again three times, but nothing worked. Each time Brian witnessed the recoil of her body off the table he knew he was closer to saying good-bye but he still held on to hope. The senior doctor made the call and asked the team to stop. He took a deep breath, closed his eyes and announced the time of death. Abby was pronounced dead. at 11:49 a.m. Hearing those final words, Brian's heart tore open and his world came cascading apart.

Abby was gone.

The gray-haired doctor, dressed in white, walked up to Brian. He reached out to take Brian's hand. "Son, I'm sorry, there was nothing more we could do. Her brain had suffered too much damage."

It was too much for him to take. "No, Abby!" Overcome by the incredible shock, Brian's legs gave out. He fell to the floor.

Abby's parents rounded the corner just as the doctor was giving Brian the news. They saw Brian collapse to the floor. Inside their souls, they knew what had been said. Running up to the stretcher that now held their daughter's lifeless body, they were helpless. Her mother cried out, "Abby! Oh, my baby girl, Abby!"

Her father reached down to hold his little girl. The instant shock of what had just happened hit them hard. Both parents were lost in the moment and their emotions. They stood there holding their daughter in their arms. Brian looked up from the floor just a few feet away; he struggled to get himself up. Standing to his feet he felt lightheaded the room was spinning but somehow he made his way over and reached out to comfort them.

Al turned away from his daughter. He saw Brian standing there. "Oh, Brian, I'm sorry. She loved you. Brian, you were Abby's one and only true love."

Prior to meeting Abby, being with her and finally falling in love, life had not been overly kind to Brian. Now, in the blink of an eye, during what seemed like an innocent outing, he had lost the one settling force that enabled him to keep it all together. He lost love. He lost acceptance. Inside, Brian felt like he had lost himself.

The three of them stood together, holding each other, they stood next to Abby. Brian leaned towards Abby's now still body. Tears were running down his cheeks. It was hard for him to breathe. "Abby, I'm sorry this happened to you. I love you and I will always love you." He then leaned forward and placed a gentle kiss on her cheek.

As Brian and her family said their final goodbyes one of the medical attendants who fought to save her life pulled the white blanket with the pale blue trim over Abby's face. It was finished.

Brian's life had been anything but simple. For someone so young, he had faced many challenges. He had lived through the breakup and relocation of his family. Brian survived the apparent rejection at the hand of his father. He adapted to the lower social class of a one income family. He overcame loneliness and isolation of always being a bit odd. He dealt with feeling like an outcast when he did not fit into the status or popularity driven social cliques of high school. All of those setbacks, those challenges would pale in comparison to the mountainous task he faced trying to move forward without Abby in his life.

CHAPTER 2

Brian's Story

Brian grew up in a somewhat unconventional setting. His parents divorced when he was 10 years old. Divorce today by National Statistics is pretty common, but in the late-eighties, it was still a bit taboo. Raised in a small town just a stone's throw from his elementary school he was one of the popular kids in the neighborhood. Everyone knew his family and his family was friendly with everyone. When it was time to choose teams for a pick-up game of street ball, or when it was time to go exploring the woods around his home he was on the A-list and one of the first chosen. Brian had many friends, his days were spent enjoying many childhood adventures.

The dirt roads, a fire station and the small woods that surrounded his home were comfortable. These surroundings provided the perfect atmosphere for raising a child. It was common for kids to be out swimming or fishing in the morning, riding bikes after lunch and chasing lightning bugs at night.

Brian wasn't the smartest kid in class. He struggled a bit with spelling but made good grades just the same. He had a girlfriend; her name was Susan. He called her Suzy. They had a lot in common, but mostly he liked to hang out with her. Brian was always happiest, felt the most comfortable when she was around.

It always bothered him that he was one of the smaller kids in his class. Even with that minor disadvantage, he found success at elementary level sports. He had a good arm, throwing a nearly perfect spiral or tossing the hardball farther and faster than anyone else. When he was not throwing the ball to others he could catch about anything thrown his way. Brian was also pretty fast a foot.

It was during the 4th grade that his school held a spring track-and-field event. From the moment he first heard about the competition over the crackling PA system following morning announcements he could not wait until the big day. He ran in and won the 50-yard dash. Wanting to impress his family he was overwhelmed with joy when he brought home a blue ribbon. Brian could not wait to show the ribbon to his father. His father promised to be at the event, but on race day he could not make it after accepting an overtime shift at the local assembly plant. Beaming with pride his mother hung the simple award on the refrigerator. To Brian, it was the equivalent of an Olympic gold medal.

The neighborhood Brian spent the first 10 years of his life in was so typical middle-class America that Norman Rockwell could have chosen it for a cover of the *Saturday Evening Post*. The best attribute of his hometown was that it was a welcoming and family friendly neighborhood. Families knew each other and the community helped each other. There were spring neighborhood cookouts, 4th of July horseshoe events and end of the summer bonfires. Normal was a family growing up together and sticking out the hard times no matter what the circumstances. Brian's normal, along with his family structure would forever change one summer.

His parents grew up in the late "1950s America" when established expectations were that after high school you found a job and then you got married. For Brian's father, that meant factory work assembling locomotives and marrying a girl he grew fond of after a brief stint in the United States Marines.

The job required the young couple to relocate to the shores of Lake Erie, the Northwest section of Pennsylvania, in the third largest city in the state. Erie was a town named for the lake and the native people that lived there. The couple settled initially on the East side in a small two story on Second Street. Within a year, they were parents. A daughter came first followed two years later when Brian was born. His mother would be a housewife and stay at home mom. Before Brian was in kindergarten the family moved to a new home in a little town called McKean. This young community of classic America ranch style homes and two story colonials was home until the 4th grade. Then as the school year came to a close his life changed in a way many had not foreseen.

Her name was Nancy. His mother was a fraternal twin, although she looked nothing like her twin brother, who was older by three minutes. She also had two sisters, one older and one younger. As Brian matured and understood more about life, he often wondered if his mother left home early, she would have been 17, to escape the middle-child syndrome. Or she may have chosen to walk down the aisle to get away from a mother who ruled the home with an iron fist. He thought it also reasonable that his mother married to get away from a demanding home life.

Richard, Brian's father may have married to escape some past demons. The man who would have been Brian's grandfather abandoned the family when Richard was a very young boy. Brian's father was raised by a mean, angry at the world Scotsman, who took much of his own displeasure with the world out on the step kids. This harsh environment may have been why his father had such a hard time relating to his own young family. Those formative years may have explained why the young husband had a drinking problem and maybe why he was never around when Brian needed him. Whatever the reasons this rejection hurt Brian in a most personal way. They were never close. Even though, Brian respected and loved the man, there was no deep bond. Although they did not have much in common, nor share many common interests.

The promise of a new life lured both of Brian's parents to run away and get married. They married young. They eloped during a getaway weekend to the Pocono Mountains of Pennsylvania and a visit to a little wedding chapel. Brian remembered a small black and white photo of the young couple. They were all smiles sitting at a dining room table with a small wedding cake in front of them. Those smiles turned into distress over the span of 10 years. With the serious conflict in the marriage, it became obvious that a picture-perfect life wasn't going to materialize from the small 3 x 5 framed photograph.

Richard stopped coming home. There were fights in the middle of the night, wrecked cars, and broken hearts. There were times when Brian and his older sister Jodi were rustled out of bed often late at night. "We have to pick up your father from another bar, he can't drive," his mother would explain. There were times that his father promised to spend time with his son only to get called into to work, have an appointment come up or something more important to tend to. Broken promises, forgotten fishing trips and the lack of any bonding left a long term void in the young boys' life. To a young son who thought the world of his dad, Brian did not understand why his father did not want to spend time with him.

Then one day, the other neighbor kids were no longer allowed to play with him. Brian noticed that the older kids and the other parents talked under their breath and pointed his way. Then the "D" word became part of the conversations. His mother explained to him what divorce meant. He really only understood that he would be living in a new home, in another neighborhood, and without his father. At first, it sounded exciting. Then he asked about his friends. He was in the fourth grade and it was supposed to be just another school year as the realtor sign was placed in the front yard.

Brian was never sure if his father saw the blue ribbon he won at the school track meet. It got thrown away when his parents sold the house, his mother packed up their possessions and moved out. A lot of his stuff, toys, balls, comic books and model airplanes got tossed in the trash.

Some other things, games, and fishing equipment were packed in boxes with the hopes that he would see them again. He never did. At times Brian felt like much of himself was packed away or tossed out with the garbage.

The family dog, Belle a sporty beagle, was another casualty. Brian was always close to the family pet, at times he joked Belle was his best friend. That statement was more true than false. Unfortunately, just like his G.I. Joes and slot car race set, one day he came home from school and Belle was gone. The family dog was never seen again. He asked his mother where Belle went; he was never given a straight or truthful answer. Brian always felt responsible, he always felt like he let his friend down and that always bothered him.

With the divorce, the kids went with their mother, as was the custom. There was a court ordered and agreed upon visitation plan. His father sank deeper into a life of drinking and isolation. They moved from a middle-class home in a country neighborhood to a trailer court on the west side of town, a stone's throw from Lake Erie. Nestled between a vintage amusement park and a drive-in theater. This location looked inviting from the outside but was not an ideal setting to host a young family. Many of the residences spent time on both sides of the tracks. This provided a challenging environment in which to raise an, in effect, fatherless family.

Within the course of that first summer, Brian went from being the kid everyone wanted to play with, the kid with the cool friends, to the child no one knew. Dealing with a single-parent home was tough. Being left out of the social interactions of the neighborhood was much harder. Brian began to feel isolated and more comfortable on his own. One constant during the long lonely summers days was that he always found a stray dog to befriend. Maybe it was the dogs finding him. Brian had the most fun and felt the most comfortable with his station in life when he had a four-legged playmate to hang out with. Unfortunately, that did not last long. With the extra burden, they placed on the limited family income the dogs only hung around until his mother shooed them away.

The years between fourth grade and his senior year in high school were filled with an increasing number of lonely days and nights. There were relocations every two to three years as they tried to stay one foot ahead of the bill collectors. The constant moves did not help his self-esteem or his standing in any established neighborhood pecking order. Along with the decline in friendships, a drop in social status affected his ability to fit in. Brian went from being an average middle-class child to being one of the poor kids in a well-to-do school district. Looking back at some of the challenges he faced growing up, any outsider may have marveled at how balanced he turned out given his circumstances.

Brian wasn't a perfect kid. As with any young boy, if you leave them alone with enough free time on their hands they will surely get into something. Brian had free time. He pretty much raised himself. The local police never showed up on his doorstep, although NASA may have wanted to talk to him about the time he attempted to launch a mouse into outer space. Then there may have been that time when a little bit of mischief, a box of laundry detergent and the water log ride ended up causing some excitement and confusion at the local amusement park. For the most part, Brian stayed out of serious trouble. He focused his hours alone on building models, collecting football cards and watching too much middle-class family drama and comedy television.

The years rolled over on the calendar as they do. The next thing his mother knew, Brian was a teenager. He was quiet, friendly and well adjusted. Maybe a bit slow to fit in, but he had no outstanding emotional or social issues. He had no more hang ups than the average young man his age.

Brian's mother was not an overly affectionate person. She tried the best she could to provide a stable home environment. Working at near minimum wage it was always a battle to make ends meet. Brian's sister Jodi was the first to crack under the increased pressure of a divorced family. She no longer wanted to live in a broken home and decided to move in with relatives, an aunt and uncle from Pittsburgh. This changed his mother's outlook on life, she felt rejected, abandoned and incompetent. Brian rallied around her when she slipped emotionally. He told her they would make it. He tried to be there for his mother. He tried to be a steady force within the home. This change in the family dynamics after the divorce caused him to grown up and mature much sooner than most boys his age.

He still got into trouble typical of a young boy, but when tempted to cross the line which could cause a serious incident, Brian always choose to go home. He just could not bring himself to add more heartbreak to his mother's life.

The mother and son combination stuck together, they rode out the storm and kept each other sane. There were good times, a trip to Sea World, and bad times, the time the electricity got shut off for a week. The pair bounced from an old trailer court next to a drive-in to a rental home and they finally purchased a 25-year-old trailer home of their own. Mostly they tried to keep the lights on, the heater fueled and some semblance of food in the house. It was the two of them against the world. The small family unit had few interactions with other families, select friends or the infrequent visitation from his father. Aside from his mother Brian felt abandon. His mother tried to explain that his father did indeed love his son. She tried to explain that some people just have a hard time demonstrating their feelings. Unfortunately, Brian's father's words and actions did much to undermine this defense.

On his father's side, Brian quickly became aware that there were more important things in life than a father spending time with his son. His father found it hard to keep up a relationship. Instead, he turned to sitting in bars drinking away his free time. During the few visitations that did take place, Brian often found himself sitting on a stool at the local American Legion or some random bar on the wrong side of town. These days were filled with eating Slim Jims, drinking Ginger Ale, watching Saturday morning cartoons and ABC's Wide World of Sports until the manager kicked them out because Brian was under aged. Pennsylvania had a strict law that minors, those under 21, could not be in bars or Taverns after 9 p.m. The rest of the evening would be spent watching old war movies as his father fell asleep. This was hardly an activity that would keep a young boy's attention.

Brian also felt worthless and unvalued by his father. When his father would pick him up the arguments with his mother over financial support were a constant. Brian never remembered his mother asking for more than the court ordered $17.50 a week child support. Although he would not have blamed her if she had. Brian knew first-hand how far that amount went in an inflation raided economy. His memories from these heated conversations were that of his father pointing out with passion that he was not going to pay one cent more. Somehow that monetary value set in his mind what his personal worth was in the eyes of the world and the most important person in his life. His dad.

From one missed visitation to another, over time life without his father became the norm. Within the first couple of years, his father stopped coming around altogether. Brian once spent the entire weekend looking out his bedroom window waiting for his father's bronze colored car to make its way down Peninsula Drive. It never showed up as he watched car after car roll by for two solid days. His mother tried to comfort him and explain away the disappointment but his soul was crushed. This rejection created a hole in Brian's heart. This emptiness shaped his identity and impacted a good portion of his life. It was the after-effects of this rejection that kept Brian on the fringes of many relationships.

With his male peers, he was never on the A-list; he was good enough to play with if everyone else was busy or on vacation. Likewise, Brian never got invited to the parties never asked to be part of the social circles. He was never picked first to join in on a pick-up game of football. He really never fit in anywhere after the divorce.

Brian loved to play football. Much of the time he was left to play catch by himself. Many after-school and weekend hours were spent throwing the ball around. To simulate a passing drill, he would attempt passes with a random tree as his intended wide receiver. He worked tirelessly until he could hit a specific location, either a discolored spot of bark or an outcropping of a branch. In junior high school, he tried out for the junior varsity football team. Brian did well in the position skills and could run reasonably fast. The coaches clocked him at five seconds flat in the 50-yard dash. His downfall was he knew nothing of conditioning or pacing.

Everything Brian did was at maximum speed, a full dead-on run. At a full-on sprint, he could not make it around the track the required four laps when Coach Lane made the team run a mile after practice for punishment. When he pulled up short, the coach furious that he quit running, kicked him off the team. Disappointed, embarrassed and dejected Brian turned in his football gear. Reluctantly he told his mother he was no longer on the team. He could hear the disappointment in her voice. As with the security of a traditional loving family, Brian's dream of playing football ended up on the scrap heap. Likewise, success around the social circle of high school was a long way off.

Around girls, Brian felt secure in a group environment. In a setting that wasn't so personal, he found it easy to join in during a conversation. He could deliver a joke or even flirt with one of the girls that caught his eye. But one-on-one, Brian was shy and quiet. He became tongue-tied and at times a bit awkward. In a more personal setting, he found it difficult to make conversations. The few times that he was able to break through those barriers, gaining the courage to ask a girl to be his steady, the normal reply was the line that no boy wanted to hear: "Let's be friends." Some of the girls were cruel in their rejection. One girl tossed the well-prepared note declaring his feelings back at his feet while another pretended she never got it. He often felt alone, isolated and at a loss for where his life was headed. Inside he wondered if he would ever fit in, or meet the girl of his dreams.

His life had been one of unmatched school boy crushes and rejection. What he knew of male-female relationships he learned watching the teenage dramas on the after-school specials, romantic sitcoms, and re-runs of 1970s family dramas. What he understood of father-son relationships he learned while watching reruns of *Brady Bunch, My Three Sons,* and *The Cosby Show.* Compared to those 30-minute snapshots of life, with built-in laugh tracks, in which everyone loved and supported one another, he found any kind of acceptance hard to come by.

Then it was the first day of eleventh grade English. She walked into the classroom catching his eye from the very first instant he saw her.. He had seen her before from afar in Junior High, but never really talked to her or got to know her. He tried not to stare. His heart raced as she took up a seat right behind his. She tapped him on the shoulder as she sat down and said "Hello, I'm Abby" With blood pressure reaching new heights and his skin feeling flush somehow he was able to carry on a conversation all the while small-scale volcanic eruptions went off within his chest. When the bell rang at the end of class Brian knew he had met a girl he liked very much.

Her name was Abigail. She liked to be called Abby. She was a bright, easy to like, humble girl who was down-to-earth. For any teenage boy, Abby was also very easy to look at. She had that natural "girl-next-door look" that so many struggled to pull off. For Abby, it was easy and effortless. Brian was always surprised that a girl like her would even talk to him. He found it easy to make conversations with her. They sat together in the row of desks closest to the door, the row positioned furthest from their teacher, Mrs. Miller. This position explained why by the end of the school year, Abby, normally a straight-A, roll student, nearly failed the class. It certainly changed the course of Brian's life.

In fifth-period English, Brian should have been learning about grammar and sentence structure. Instead, he learned about Abby. What started out as tentative flirtation, turned into something much more. Their first conversations centered on discovering each other's favorite bands, movies, colors, or their opinions on the "cool kids." These discussions eventually grew into a deeper broader connection. Brian enjoyed talking with Abby about their lives away from the confines of the high school social structure. Over the course of the year, the two shared their ideas on life. They shared their dreams for the days after high school. When randomly Brian asked Abby how she saw her life in five years, he was shocked, floored and overwhelmed when she replied, "With you silly." They found they had a lot in common.

What mattered most to a young man struggling to find his place within the dynamics of his senior year in high school was that they liked and deeply cared for one another. Brian believed he had found someone to share his heart. He felt that he'd found acceptance. He hoped he'd found someone who would love him back. When Abby confirmed this, everything in his world changed. Almost immediately, having Abby in his life, Brian felt a surge of self-confidence and self-worth. These two feelings had escaped him for many years, really they had escaped him for all of his life.

For Brian, the hours spent in high school no longer resembled a prison sentence, a sentence where you had weekends off for work-release. No longer did the hallways of McDowell High School feel like a prison cell and or passageways leading to the executioner. Now Brian looked forward to his time at school. He felt better about himself and the outlook for his future. The school was no longer a place to try and hide while the required five and half hours ticked off the clock. Abby's smiling face and her pretty eyes greeted him every day. The fact that she took an interest in him changed everything. The handful of friends he had, noticed a difference right away. He was more outgoing, more confident and his teachers noticed that his daily attendance improved. Brian's path in life was changing.

From the day Abby told Brian she liked him the two were nearly inseparable. Over the course of their relationship, nourished by a deeper connection than he had ever known, Brian felt loved, accepted and valued. Under this positive influence, he grew into a caring and fun loving young man. Confident and happy, he was always up for an adventure. The two of them were always laughing and getting out of life all it had to offer. Life seemed to have finally dealt Brian an even hand. The remaining school year flew by and graduation was right around the corner. Counting down the days until the next stage of their lives would unfold, Brian and Abby were very happy together.

For his graduating class, the next chapter in their lives would bring a lot of unknowns. Brian and Abby's relationship had reached a point that they may not have known what career they might choose or what part of the country they may live in but both were confident that no matter what direction their future turned, they would face it together.

After graduating from high school their dates turned into weekend adventures. Weekend outings turned into vacations and vacations into planning the next stage of their lives. As the months rolled into years, their relationship fueled a deep passion that overflowed into all other areas of Brian's life.

Others saw running as a struggle, a form of punishment or the tedious conditioning required of their sport. To Brian, running was freedom. Running was an open door to adventure and a calm place in a busy, hectic and often misunderstood world.

Brian was never the most athletic student in high school. He could keep himself from falling below the competitive water line, but he was never the star player in any organized sport. He never won the game, hit the home run or anchored the victory lap. After the disappointment with the junior varsity football team, he tried out for the track team the following spring.

The track coach needed a middle-distance runner and noticed that although Brian lacked conditioning, he had potential. With the coaches' support and encouragement he made the varsity track squad. He ran the 800 meters and 1-mile run. Brian did his best, but those distances were not his niche. He enjoyed the long training runs much better than the shorter race lengths. Brian enjoyed running with the team and found some limited success.

Brian learned about pacing, conditioning and training plans. Once he understood how to run and how to pace himself, he enjoyed running more than anything else, athletically. Growing into the sport Brian found some success, placing as high as second in the 1-mile finals during an inter-conference high school track meet. He knew there had to be something more to this.

After high school, Brian continued to run without being forced into an ill-fitting competitive category. Free to run and race as he pleased, he chose to enter some of the local 5 and 10-kilometer events commonly found on most Saturday mornings. During this time, a deep love for the sport developed. This love for the sport calmed Brian's soul, but it did not translate into being an elite runner.

Brian felt at home racing. He enjoyed the competition but never won his age group. He was happy to place in the top 10 percent of finishers. Then, almost by accident, Brian discovered that the longer he ran, the better he performed. Marathon, ultra-marathons, and extreme distances suited his natural abilities. For someone who once found failure trying to complete four laps around the high school track, Brian realized a gift, a passion, a talent he never knew he had.

For Brian, the distances in excess of the marathon distance of 26.2 miles became more about the experience than the finishing time or placement on the leaderboard. Once mastering these extreme distances, Brian eventually found that he loved the adventurous side of these events. If running 26, 50 or 100 miles was extreme, running that distance over a mountainous trail must surely be the ultimate challenge. This trait attracted him towards adventure running. In this exaggerated form of running, he could not only live the run but in his mind's eye, he could see a story developing within the run. Telling this story and relaying the experience became more important than simply logging miles. Just as his talent for tackling extreme distances came as a surprise, discovering that other people enjoyed reading his tales came as an unexpected bonus.

Writing was another area where Brian found limited success in high school. In the structured academic lessons, he felt confined and unable to express himself. This reality was emphasized by the ever present telltale red-penciled marks, critical words, and notations on his assignments. In his own mind, he could never understand how his teachers missed the message within his story. It perplexed him how they missed the true point behind his writings. Perhaps the teachers were unable to see the written narrative, the story being told, behind their intellectual need to find faults in his grammar, sentence structure, and spelling. Brian enjoyed writing but in the high school classroom environment, he found it stifling.

Free from the confines of the academic world, Brian was able to explore writing and expressing himself without the rigid rules of high school English 101. Not professionally trained or even educated beyond his brief college career, on a dare, he submitted one of his essays to a running magazine. Nine months later, he was surprised when a plain white business-sized envelope appeared in the mail. Inside was a contract from a national magazine who wanted to publish his work. This first success was followed up by other submissions and other articles being published. Eventually came a request from *Trail Running & Beyond (TRB)* magazine to work as a freelance contributor.

It wasn't long before Brian held a feature segment with *TRB* magazine. It was always a surprise to him that readers were entertained by his writings. His two passions mixed together perfectly, one feeding off the other. Brian would escape on a running adventure, write about the experience and the magazine would publish it. It almost seemed too easy to him. He wasn't an elite writer. Brian's works would never displace the likes of Miller, Hemingway or Clancy, but he was talented enough at stringing words together to make a modest if not a decent living doing what he loved. Brian's life after high school was the model of everything he could have ever asked for. Life was good.

CHAPTER 3

Her Name was Abby

When they first met, Abby was not a long distance runner. She enjoyed being fit, ran cross country in high school and had a passion for proper nutrition and exercise. Although she enjoyed going for a good run, she admittedly was not one of those "crazy types" who ran for hours on end. Outside of her athletic pursuits, she was a member of the honor roll and believed in making a difference in the community. Abby also had a true concern for the lives of others with whom she came in contact with.

Abby was the only daughter in what would be viewed as an iconic All-America family. Her father and mother had been high school sweethearts. They enjoyed a three-year courtship before tying the knot in a traditional large family wedding. Married 25 years. By all accounts, they had never said a cruel word to each other or spent a night apart since saying "I do" on a spring afternoon. They had two children, Abby, who was two years removed from their first anniversary, her brother followed two years later and one dog, a spunky little Jack Russell. Her family lived in the same red brick cape cod home at the same address the majority of her life. The Tudor-styled red brick two story with an attached two car garage set back on a half-acre lot included even the traditional white picket fence.

Her father was a white-collar professional, although he did not start out that way. Right out of high school he got hired on with a paper mill as unskilled labor. His first assignment on the operations floor, was running a press mill. His drive and determination did not go unnoticed, he eventually made it to the professional offices in the "head shed" working special projects for the plant manager. He was one of the very few who worked in this main office building without a major college degree. Even with his success climbing the corporate ladder, he never forgot where he came from. His life was solid and predictable. He went to work, came home on time, loved his wife and invested his time, energy and love in his children.

Her mother worked full-time as well but also kept a near-perfect home. Abby's mom spent her days as an office executive for a local law firm and her nights tending to her family. Although not expected to, she had meals prepared at almost the same time every day. She was busy with her church and in the community. This was the kind of stereotypical all-American family Brian dreamed about being a part of.

Over the months, as Brian and Abby's relationship flourished, Brian became a welcomed part of Abby's family. He was included in many family functions and spent most of his free time hanging out around their home. He felt the warmth, acceptance, and trust from her family. To repay that faith Brian worked tirelessly to fulfill Abby's dreams and ensure she felt valued, loved and safe. The connection these two had was easily apparent to anyone who saw them together. They were in love and their lives fit together well.

After high school, while Brian ran, worked part-time and began writing, Abby was earning her degree in sports nutrition. She was a smart girl who was able to keep her life together effortlessly, one of the many traits Brian admired in her. When needed, Abby helped Brian maintain his personal affairs above the water line. They lived apart. Neither of them believed in living together until after they were married. The couple shared a core belief in the creator God and lived their lives as witnesses to him. They attended church and volunteered in the community.

When she was not tending to her studies, Abby found time to work with her JV cross country team as a volunteer coach and enjoyed giving back to her former school. She relished the opportunity to interact with the girls and delighted in seeing them develop into better runners and more importantly into mature, self-confident young ladies. Abby developed many relationships within the team and the girls spoke highly of her.

Outside of work and errands associated with living two separate lives Brian and Abby spent very little time apart. The couple enjoyed going to movies, fancy dinners and watching the sunset off of Bundy Beach on the peninsula. They also enjoyed walking around the mall and just hanging out. About the only time, they spent apart was when Brian went for a long run. Slowly even that was changing.

Abby was defiantly having a positive impact on Brian's life. He knew that and everyone connected to his life saw the change. His mother mentioned it often that Abby brought out the best in him. Brian was also having an influence over Abby's habits.

Reluctantly at first, losing a playful bet, she ventured out on some long runs with Brian. Her cross country running was accomplished over less than challenging groomed trails or on converted rails-to-trails paths. It surprised even her when she found enjoyment in the more demanding and technical single track trails that Brian introduced her to. Abby fell in love with the challenge and freedom this new form of fitness offered her.

Prior to trail running, she kept in shape training with the cross country girls, taking aerobics classes or on the spin bikes at the gym. Abby found herself drawn to the half-marathon distance of 13.1 miles. With a quick and easy gait, she was surprised at the speed held captive in her legs. Normally not a competitive person, when on the trails or in "race mode" Abby found a fire that did not want anyone thinking they got the best of her. It did not take her long to become a regular on the trails and at local races.

A natural, she was a gifted runner. In her second race, Abby made a splash. It was a women's half marathon, run over semi-improved trails and fire roads within a state park. Brian knew this race was going to be tough. The course foundation was made of loose dirt, sand, and gravel. Compounding those conditions was the fact that it had rained the night before.

Sending Abby off to the starting line he assured her that he would see her at the halfway point and at the finish. Brian was excited to be supporting Abby out on the race course as she had done so many times for him. This allowed him to enjoy a race from the other side of the ropes.

As the race progressed Brian stood anxiously on the side of the trail, tapping his right foot in the soggy soil. He noted the amount of mud that formed from this simple action and knew instantly that the trails would be a mess. The girls would be running in some tough conditions. Time dragged on as he waited for the first pack of runners to make their way out of the woods and into the open. Then suddenly the lead girl broke out into the clearing.

Within seconds two more girls running shoulder to shoulder came into the clearing. Brian's eyes became as wide as saucers as he noted Abby was the third girl out of the woods. His heart began to pound as if in overdrive, he readied her water bottle while he positioned himself to hand her a quick drink. "You're doing great Abby, throw it away when you're done and RUN GIRL RUN!" He shouted out, overly excited from seeing his girl near the front. He knew she was fast but he also knew she lacked the racing experience to beat some of the local favorites. He was worried she might not be able to position herself correctly. He was worried she would get boxed in. His original plan was to make his way to the finish and be there to help her at the end, but Brian knew a short cut.

Once done meeting her hydration needs and cheering Abby on Brian ducked into the woods and raced for the nine-mile loop. At this sweeping turn, there would be another opportunity to see her. With the pace he knew the lead pack was running, Brian wasted no time.

Arriving at the nine-mile loop, Brian was ready for anything. Was Abby still in contact with the lead group or did she fall off the back of the pack? His questions would soon be answered as a rustle of sounds approached. From where he was standing he could hear their labored breathing before he saw the first placed girl appear around the bend, break into the clear and come into view. Brian was not prepared for what he saw next. Abby was in the lead and the second place girl was 15 yards behind her. Abby raced down the trail at full speed and turned sharply into the looping left-hand turn. Her eyes caught Brian's...nothing was said she simply locked eyes with his and smiled. Caught off guard, Brian snapped back, "stop smiling girl and run, you've got the lead."

As Abby went out of view, Brian dashed off the trail and into the woods again, he had to make it to the finish line before the race was over. Bounding from the trail surface, over jagged rocks and around exposed tree roots Brian took advantage of some paths he blazed over many of his freelance training runs. He knew the trails here like the back of his hand but he also knew it would be close. He reasoned if he really poured on the coals he could make the finish line right before the lead girl broke out onto the fire road. From the fire road entrance, it was a one hundred yard sprint to the finish.

The fire road was lined with spectators as Brian sprung out of the woods and onto the road. Dirt, mud and leaves were stuck to his running pants, one of the spectators who saw him come out of the woods asked, "Who are you running from a bear?"

Brian replied, "No not a bear, I'm trying to stay ahead of my girlfriend, she leading this race and I'm not going to miss her finish."

Just as he caught his breath two figures appeared dead center in the middle of the road. By all appearances, the girls were running at high speed. Brian could tell by the familiar silhouette that the one on the left was Abby and it looked like she was behind.

Both runners bore signs of just how hard fought the race had been. Their faces were focused, determined and spattered with mud and trail debris. It was apparent that Abby had not spent the entire race in the lead. The telltale signs of following another runner on a wet day were readily apparent. Abby ran in her familiar green race shoes which were barely recognizable, the preceding miles left them soaked and covered in grime and muck. Her race kit of a navy blue mid-thigh compression shorts, borrowed from the varsity team and a light green high-rise singlet was spattered with stains of mud and grit. None of that mattered, whatever fight Abby had been through left her battling for the lead with just yards to go.

Stride after stride the two came closer to the finish. Fifty yards from pay dirt, they were shoulder to shoulder, neither had been able to pull away from the other. The girl Abby was locked in battle with was one of the local favorites. Slightly taller than Abby with a slender build and a long stride. Abby was matching her stride for stride. Brian was concerned that Abby's competition had more racing experience. He was concerned that she might be waiting to pull a finishing kick on Abby. Thirty yards from the finish they were locked in rhythmic motion each matching the others footfall, arm swing, and leg turnover. If unaware that they were in a competitive race, you would have thought it was a perfectly choreographed run scene out of some Hollywood action movie.

Only a single step separated them. The girls were intertwined in a heated battle for the lead. Fifteen yards from the finish they passed close enough that Brian could see right into Abby's eyes. Those brown eyes that he found so inviting were in a stone cold stare fixed on the ground right in front of her. Brian called out, "Run Abby…Dig deep you got this!" The familiar sound of his voice broke her concentration. Abby cocked her head slightly to the side, enough to look his way. Making eye contact she winked at him. Startled, shocked and amazed he thought she was crazy. Abby then in one transition of her leg turnover stretched out and lengthened her stride. In one quick twitch of her long and lean leg muscles, she pulled ahead and into the lead. Her competitor could not match the move. The race was over.

In shock and awe, Brian stood along the road mumbling to himself, "here I was worried about her and she had it in the bag. What a girl!"

Abby crossed the finish line five yards in front of second place. Brian ran as fast as he could to meet her still overwhelmed at her performance. "Abby you won," he called out as he slung his arms around her waist and lifted her off her tired and very muddy feet. Instantly Brian noticed how good she felt in his arms. Today as always, he was so proud of her. "I Love you, Abby!"

Abby was out of breath, weary and happy that she won the race. Once back on her feet, she walked over to congratulate her competitors on a hard fought race. They were all very gracious. As she walked away they commented to one another "we are going to have to battle her for a long time to come." Abby ran back to Brian's arms and thanked him for being there for her.

"I wouldn't be anywhere else, Abby. You are everything to me." Brian paused for a moment. "But no more winking at me during a race, you're going to kill me."

Then parting from her normal conservative nature Abby gave Brian a long, passionate and very muddy kiss.

Afterward, Brian commented, "Abby, we make a pretty good team."

"We sure do, your kind of stuck with me Mister."

CHAPTER 4

Going for a Run

It was a Sunday evening, a perfect ending to a weekend filled with laughter, hand-holding, and smiles. Abby and Brian had spent nearly the entire time together. As Brian drove Abby home the couple talked about their lives, his writing, her college courses and her racing plans after her first win on the mud-soaked trails six weeks earlier. When they arrived at her home neither one of them wanted the evening to end. The pair continued to make small talk until Brian told Abby he couldn't wait for the day when they would not have to say good night. The mood was electric he leaned in to kiss her and tried to say goodnight. She would not let the moment part so easily. Abby turned it into one of those playful goodnights that took forever as neither one of them wanted to say the final words of the evening or turn and walk away.

Once home he called Abby around 11 p.m.

Abby picked up the phone on the second ring and playfully without confirming who was on the other end she asked. "You miss me already?"

"Yes, I do," Brian replied. "Abby. Instead of waiting until after work to get in our run, why don't we go out to Church Hill Road in the morning?" He paused to clear his throat. "I need to get in my 20-mile long run. We can drop off your car at the old gas station. You can ride back with me and then run a quick 10 miles with me out to your car. Once you're done you can then jump in and go home. I'll meet you when I'm done and after I've cleaned up."

The route picked was a familiar one. Away from the hustle and bustle of the small town yet, near enough where it was an easy drive to get to.

Brian called Abby early the next morning. She always needed a little help to get moving in the morning. On the other hand, he was an early bird.

"Morning, sunshine. You're still running with me this morning, right?"

Half-awake. Her voice muffled and barely audible. Abby responded, "Yeah, but don't be so happy about it mister early bird."

Brian played along. "Well, all right then, Missy, get your coffee. I'll meet you at the gas station in an hour."

That was one of the few areas Brian and Abby's vibes did not line up. Abby was a coffee nut some would call her a coffee snob. Brian had never had a cup. He always told her he preferred his drinks cold and that hot drinks did nothing for him.

"All right, you better not be smiling, Mr. Happy Face" Abby said back.

"Do you need another wake-up call?" there was a long silent pause. "Love you, Abby." Brian chuckled.

"Love you more." Abby got in the final jab and then hung up.

Brian arrived early at the old run-down gas station. He sat in his truck listening to music while fidgeting with his running gear. It was around 6:30. "Abby should be rolling in around 7," he thought to himself. He

Brian Burk

didn't mind being there alone. This quiet, peaceful time of the day provided an opportunity to relax. Brian found solace listening to music while he got his mind right for the upcoming run.

Today's long run would be run at his goal pace for an upcoming marathon. Brian hoped Abby's speed would help keep the opening miles fast and anchored on his target. He gazed out of the truck's front windshield. His eyes caught sight of a bird, maybe a hawk, flying across the sky above an open field. The sun was just cresting as beams of light were breaking thru the pre-dawn sky. As the sun rose it cast an orange to pink hue on the horizon. The temperature was going to be mild. The message center on the dash of his truck told him it was 52 degrees. Combining that with the forecast and it looked as if it was going to be a clear day. Brian loved mornings like this. It was his favorite part of the day. When asked why his reply was always that each new day was filled with promise. He loved adventures, he loved being on the move, but he treasured the quiet times of life as well.

The morning stillness was broken as a car rolled into the parking area. Brian heard the commotion and looked over his shoulder to see what was going on. A slight dust cloud kicked up as Abby's car pulled into the parking lot. She was right on the nose, 7 a.m. The car fit the drivers' personality perfectly, a shiny red Volkswagen Jetta. As Abby stepped out of her car, Brian called out, "Hey, you. We need to stop meeting like this, people might talk."

"Hey there yourself. They do talk. They say you can't keep up with me this morning," Abby snapped back with her trademark little girl grin.

Brian wasn't sure if she meant it or not. "All right, Ms. Speedy Pants, get in. Let's get going." A pause hung in the air. "Oh, by the way, I love you." He handed her a small collection of blue and white wildflowers he had picked on his way to meet her. It was blue.

Abby climbed into his truck. "Thank you, you're sweet." Quickly she slid over and placed a little kiss on his check. "I still love you, more," Abby playfully replied.

35

The one thing Brian liked nearly as much as running was his big truck. When one of his running stories hit big, he took the money he earned and purchased a bright silver Dodge one ton dually four-wheel drive pickup. Abby thought it was overkill. Brian reminded her whenever he could that no one, at least no male in the 18 to 50-year-old demographic ever said: "I wish I had a smaller truck" when they needed it.

The two sat quietly as they drove back towards town. They were holding hands and listening to the radio. Brian was always happier when Abby was around. He glanced over and smiled. Feeling the weight of his eyes on her, she caught his gaze. "Hey, you, keep your eyes on the road."

"Yea, yea Okay, but you're so pretty, no, you're stunning this morning." They both laughed as Brian pulled the truck off the road and into a scenic lookout point. They had traveled a touch further than 10 miles from the old gas station. Once the truck came to a stop and before they both unbuckled, Brian leaned over and gave her a very nice kiss. Then they both jumped out of the truck and began to get things adjusted for their run.

After a few minutes to warm up and get all of their gear sitting right, Brian glanced over at Abby, admiring her. She was wearing a pair of black three-quarter length running tights stopping just above her knees and a teal-green performance camisole. Her hair was tied back in a sporty ponytail, stuck behind her right ear was the blue pedaled wildflower. He never got tired of looking at her and often wondered what a good-looking girl like her had seen in him.

The weather was near-perfect, a bright sky rising in the east with a cool, almost refreshing breeze. Blue skies hung overhead with barely the faint whisper of a cloud across the horizon. These were the days God made for running. "Abby, are you ready for this? Let's go out the first mile around a 8:30 pace per mile, then pick it up from there." Brian motioned for Abby to come closer, his tone turned serious. "Our goal is to make the 10-mile turn right at an hour and fifteen. You game?"

Abby, listening intently replied, "You're so cute when you get all Mister Serious, about your running, I'll get you there, buddy, you just try and keep up."

The two took off down the old double lane road heading northeast. The morning sun reflecting off the blacktop road felt good on his face. The first mile came and went effortlessly, Abby had them running right on target. Perfectly synchronized was the width and cadence of their leg turnover. "You ready to open this thing up?" Abby spoke up in-between breaths.

"Who, me?" Brian puffed back.

Abby took off, "Let's go then" she picked up the pace. With that first easy mile behind them, the next five quickly clicked off on his GPS watch. A quarter of the way into the run, the sun was rising up high in the east. The morning rays increasingly felt good. They made their way down the road running side by side, Abby on Brian's left side, her feet falling crisply on the single white line on the side of the road away from the on-coming traffic. Brian was a half-step in front and towards the center of the road.

Normally when they ran, they both chattered along like long lost friends. When there was work to be done like today, they concentrated on the task at hand and hardly a word was spoken. Then out of the blue, the silence was broken. "Abby, do you think your parents would be okay going out to dinner with us on Saturday?"

"You want to talk about this now, with my lungs ready to explode?" Abby piped back, pointing out the obvious.

He was caught off guard, just a bit. "Well, they have done so much for me and the new Italian place has just opened," Brian reasoned.

She could not understand why he would want to talk about this now. Brian's visit to a local jewelry store a month earlier would have clued in anyone watching from the outside. Abby was unaware of this visit and accepted the ill-timed conversation as, just another one of those "Brian things;" she continued to run. "Sure, I'll ask them later, Can we talk about this after the run? Okay, hot shot?" her reply would have sounded a bit testy to anyone not aware of her playful side.

After that brief exchange, the two became quiet as Brian got back to work. Near-perfect stillness surrounded them the only sound being the gripping and releasing of their running shoes on the road surface. For a long-distance runner, this familiar sound is almost comforting. The repeated cadence of a foot striking the ground was followed by the sounds of the rubber sole gripping and then pushing off from the road surface. He glanced at his GPS watch and noticed their pace. "Good running, Abby. We are right on target," Brian forced out between breaths.

Abby responded right back. "Yeah, good, thought I might have lost you." She always had a fast and keen wit to go along with her near perfect stride.

Brian noticed the perspiration that formed on Abby's forehead. Her shoulder-length blonde hair was pulled back in a ponytail that trailed behind her. Her body was graceful and lean. She was everything he had ever hoped for. Inside Brian knew his life was complete with her. Abby made him feel wanted, important and happy. For the first time in his life, he felt content. Brian's mind wandered from the effort behind his run. "How was I ever so lucky?"

Before his vision returned to the roadway in front of him, with a parting glance Brian noticed the blue wildflower tucked behind Abby's ear. He smiled as he once again returned to the repetitive nature of his feet striking the asphalt below.

The repeating cadence of their run was broken by a noise that came out of nowhere. Brian's attention was instantly diverted to the sound that was sweeping over them. The nature of this disturbance was unfamiliar; a roaring commotion, a reverberation that came up from behind. Along with the disturbing clatter, Brian sensed a change in the air pressure around them.

It all happened so fast and yet so stereotypically slow that time and space began to move frame by frame. His brain reasoned that the sounds were mechanical in nature. He could hear the rattle of metal and the drone of an accelerating engine getting closer. The vibrations from tires rolling along the road grew louder and louder. As these sounds registered his brain pieced together precisely what was going on. Instantly fear swept over and panic crept into his bones. Brian twisted his head around 180 degrees to see what was approaching from behind him. Then in a blink of an eye, he stopped dead in his tracks.

In one fleeting moment, two runners who previously had been alone on a quiet and deserted road were joined by a metallic 4,000-pound rapidly approaching monster.

Brian was a stickler for safety. When they ran on the streets he insisted they always run facing traffic, as is the proper way and that was no exception today. In front of them, the road was all clear, open, free and innocent. The few cars they had encountered this early morning were greeted with a friendly smile and a wave. Approaching drivers normally waved back giving them wide clearance. Now from behind, unseen and unexpected, a torment of unpredictable motion was coming their way.

The driver had his own issues. An older man in his late sixties, he was fighting for his life. What started out earlier in the day as an uncomfortable hot flash progressed into a heart rate that felt like a machine gun bursting off rounds within his chest cavity. As he drove towards home on this lonely road a scorching pain started running from his left ear all the way down to the tips of his fingers.

Now in the beginning stages of a massive heart attack, this man's chest seared in pain. The weight of the world felt like it was closing in on him and then as paths crossed it became too much. The man desperate to rid himself of this pain closed his eyes and lost control of his vehicle. More desperate, he was losing himself. As the intense pressure in his chest won out, his limbs stiffened and his life went dark. The unguided truck darted across the road with the accelerator pressed to the floorboards. The truck became more of an unguided missile than a mode of transportation. With an unconscious victim at the controls, the unrestrained torment bore down on them from behind.

The sound grew louder and louder. The disturbance swelled more and more intense. When Brian's natural instincts took over it was too late. The truck was nearly on top of them. He instinctively reached out to grab Abby. It all happened too fast. The front right headlight hit his left hand. The impact spun him around and tossed him aside. There was a sharp pain in his right hip as he hit the ground. The momentum caused his body to roll along the road surface tearing away patches of skin from his forearms. Suddenly he was gripped with terror as he saw the shiny chrome plated bumper first make contact with Abby's right hip and then her lower back.

The impact lifted Abby off the ground and out of her shoes. Her slight frame offered no resistance. Brian could do nothing but watch as she flew forward and into the air. His heart sank. He cried out, *"ABBY!"*

Then a tremendous sound caught Brian's attention. The truck came to rest in a drainage ditch that ran along the roadway. At near full speed, a dirt embankment was the only thing that brought the out of control mass of metal to an instant halt. The impact and sudden stop lifted the rear wheels off the ground. Brian could see that the driver impacted the front windshield. From his vantage point, Brian knew in his soul that this was bad. His focus then returned to Abby.

Her body spun around like a leaf falling from a tree. It all happened so quickly, yet the events played out frame by terrible frame. His eyes wanted to close. He did not want to be a witness to this terrible accident, but in horror, he could do nothing but watch.

Still disoriented from his own impact Brian stumbled as he tried desperately to get his body to move in Abby's direction. Try as he might, his reaction time was not nearly fast enough, he could not close the distance in time. He reached out as if he could somehow catch her.

In a bizarre twist of fate, the world seemed to stop spinning. Abby hung in midair for a brief second where everything stopped. For a moment he thought he could stop this horrific event from playing out. Beyond Brian's control, the world began to turn again.

As gravity took over, her body landed on the side of the road like a discarded doll. As she came to a rest on the shoulder of the road, the momentum caused her head to whiplash up and then back down. When her head hit the ground, the sound was unforgettable. There was a small dust cloud created by the impact. Brian heard Abby cry out and then everything around him went deathly quiet.

Back on his feet, Brian moved as fast as he could to get to Abby's side. Once there he knelt next to her. He tried to get some response. "Abby, Abby, please be okay. Honey, I love you." At first, he noticed no signs of life. She did not respond to his attempts to get her attention. His heart grew fearful. He expected the worse. Then his eyes caught movement around her chest. He noticed her breathing; he placed his hand over her heart and could feel her chest move as her lungs expanded. He quickly checked for a pulse. He found one in her wrist, despite the dire situation, there was hope. He spoke out loud, nearly as much to reassure himself as he did for Abby. "Good. You are alive. Abby, you're still with us."

Outwardly there were no apparent signs of obvious physical trauma. There were no misshaped limbs. No signs of a compound fracture and no obvious loss of blood. If it wasn't for the fact that he'd witnessed the horrific event, Brian would have thought she had just lain down to sleep along the side of the road.

At first, Abby was not responding to Brian's pleas. "Abby, please wake up, be okay. PLEASE!" Brian called out as he gently shook her, trying desperately to get a response. When it seemed liked nothing was working, Abby opened her eyes.

What happened? She asked in a soft and barely audible voice. Brian did his best to explain but as he spoke to her, Abby's eyes closed again.

Terrified, fearful and unsure what to do, he held her in his arms. He could not lose her. In Abby, he found kindness, hope, and love. His life finally had meaning and a future. He found love, the perfect love he had always dreamed about.

Finally, Brian did the only thing he could do. He held Abby in his arms, comforted her best he could and prayed to the creator God that everything would be okay. Without her, could he move on, could he ever be whole, would he ever really love again?

CHAPTER 5

Life After the Accident

Since Brian and Abby were not married, her family took care of the funeral details. They picked out the cemetery lot, they made her final arrangements and they decided what she would wear. They did their best to include Brian in everything. He appreciated their kindness. In such a case of traumatic grief, he felt for much of the process that he was a visitor watching from the outside. His mind was not focused on a casket, flower arrangements or a cemetery plot. Brian's thoughts and emotions were taxed with trying to survive the next minute, the next hour and the next day. He had planned to share the rest of his life with Abby. Brian was living each moment realizing he would never see her smiling face, look into those inviting eyes, hold her tender hand or kiss her sweet lips again.

Abby had a lot of friends, nearly all of them came to her funeral. It was a picture-perfect spring day. A slight chill was in the air with a bright sun beaming overhead. After the pastor said all the right words about the end of life, the promise of another life and meeting your savior in heaven, he read from the Bible, one of Abby and Brian's favorite passages: John 3:16 "For God so loved the world that he gave his one and only Son, that whoever believes in him shall not perish but have eternal life...."

Brian and Abby were Christians; they believed in Christ. They lived their short lives together after his ways and teachings. Knowing of Abby's faith Brian found some comfort knowing she was in heaven.

At the conclusion of the ceremony, Abby's friends and family members slowly made their way to say goodbye to her and to her family. Brian sat next to her family in the front row of mourners. Her brother was quiet and held on to his mother's hand. Her mother softly cried. Her father was brave and thanked everyone for coming. Abby's family kept up a brave front, but inside, each one was missing a large portion of who they were.

Brian sat on her father's right side. For much of the ceremony, he kept his eyesight focused on the ground in front of him or at times looking into the bright sunshine. Brian's mother sat behind him and kept her hand on his shoulder. She knew how much Abby meant to him. She had been in the best position to witness his transformation from a slightly reclusive boy into a positive and outgoing young man. She knew all of this was because of Abby's love.

As each guest said their final goodbyes, many from the running community placed running shoes, race numbers and race medals at her graveside. When Brian noticed this act of respect admiration and love, these gestures it touched his heart. He knew Abby would have appreciated the gesture. At one point, he simply turned his sights up high into the beautiful morning sky. He thought of Abby, their brief time together and despite the pain, those thoughts took him away and made him smile. He missed her so much already. In the front breast pocket of his jacket was the ring he had planned to give her. None of the visitors or her family knew of his plans for the dinner at the Italian restaurant. Nor did they know about his plans for the rest of their lives together. He carried that grief alone.

The crowd of well-wishers wanted to shake hands, give hugs and offer encouraging words. As they said their goodbyes they recounted their impressions of Abby.

"She was a great girl and full of life."

Slowly, as everyone departed from graveside all who remained were Abby's parents, her brother, and Brian.

As the four sat comforting each other, her father assured him, "We are and will always be family. We love you." Abby's father had to pause to keep the tears at bay. "Abby may be gone, but we are not."

All Brian could say was, "Thank you. I'm going to miss her…she was the only person who ever truly LOVED me." His voiced was course and broken. It was hard for him to continue. He took a deep breath and regained enough composure to finish the sentence. "I'm sure; Abby was MY one and only true love."

With the services concluded, it was time for Brian to take the first steps of his new life. Although Abby had left his world three days before, he knew this would be the first night he was truly alone. Leaving graveside, he hated the thought of going back to his small apartment to the stillness of an empty life. But inside, he knew he had to. The world was going to continue to turn. Brian knew nothing he could do would stop it or return Abby to him. Brian knew that Abby would want him to move on, to follow his dreams, and to find some peace

Brian arrived home to the eerie silence of his apartment. Although the key fit into the lock and the familiar door opened; today something was wrong. Opening the door, walking across the threshold, everything looked and felt different. Walking inside the atmosphere felt like he was stepping into someone else's life. This life was filled with despair, heartbreak, remorse and emptiness. He stopped five feet inside the doorway. The quiet hum of the appliances and the ticking of the clock on the wall were deafening. Everything was still, the room was dark and although everything sat in its rightful place, he felt out of place, he felt like nothing belonged.

Brian tried to establish some kind of routine. He tried to get his mind to disconnect from the events of that day. He tried to relax and to begin taking the necessary steps for him to accept being alone. Painfully, nothing Brian did could erase the mental images of Abby's coffin being lowered to her final resting place.

Being alone Brian was restless, nervous and uneasy, both physically and emotionally. As the hours passed he would sit in one chair for only a few moments. Then he would get agitated, jittery and get up and move to another location. Trying to break the quietness of the empty apartment, he turned on the television. The stale sound filled the room, but nothing could replace the emptiness in his heart. He finally had enough.

He had to do something productive, changing clothes; he put on a pair of black shorts, a black shirt and laced up his running shoes. Retreating to the only place he thought he could find some comfort, he decided to go for a run. Not wanting to be alone, but being all alone, he headed to the trails. The same trails they ran together. "Maybe I won't feel so alone out there," he reasoned to himself. Brian recognized it would take time, but he needed to get through this very real and very dark night. The run helped but it was only temporary solace.

Days passed and his life moved on like he knew it would. Brian tried to keep his days busy. He got back into his routine, he returned to running, he returned to writing and he tried to turn the page on this tragic chapter of his life. The nights were tough. He found himself going to bed earlier and earlier. He desired to shorten the days of depression as much as he could. He knew he could not afford to let his mind wander. Every day was a battle with his thoughts. Would anger, self-pity, depression and hopelessness win out or could he keep the negative feelings in check and stay positive? The sense of loss and loneliness threaten to drag him down a dark road full of sorrow, remorse, and guilt.

Weeks passed, Brian had spent the majority of this time alone. Other than to go to the store to pick up some necessary items or to get out and run he had not left his apartment since the services. A few of his closest friends had stopped by to see how he was doing. Some brought food others offered to hang out or go out to a movie or maybe dinner. Brian appreciated their thoughts and understood they were reaching out to him but he just was not in the mood. He was not in the right frame of mind.

When Brian did venture out he found many people who wanted to talk about "the event" as he called it or about his plans for the future. All were concerned for him and his well-being. It was clear within in their community circle just how much Abby meant to him. How much she made his life full, well-balanced and complete. They wanted to share their loss and feelings for Abby and they wanted to make sure he was okay. Understanding their concern for him, he tried to be cordial, but Brian really did not want to experience again something he could not change. He knew they meant well, we understood they were trying to lift his spirits.

To him, the outside world, life outside of his circle of loss, continued to move on and he was happy to have some work that needed his attention. His writings had always been an escape and now he needed a diversion. Still residing in his due out folder on the hard drive of his laptop was some work he hoped would be enough of a distraction to provide some sense of retreat from a world he did not want to be part of. *"The Essence of Trail Running"* was an article he had promised his editors for their next issue and the deadline was approaching. The magazine publishers offered to extend the due date but the last thing he wanted was more time. More time to think, more time to struggle with his emotions. He did not need more time. He thought getting back to work would help take his mind off the thoughts and images that haunted him.

Although he wanted to get back to some sense of a normal life. He wanted to get to his work, to a life that did not focus on loss and it was not going to be an easy road. Brian soon found it was hard to make words appear on the computer screen. His mind was overflowing with ideas, story lines and half-written sentences. Yet when it came time to organize his thoughts, when it came time to quiet his mind to make sense of the jumbled stockpile of ideas he drifted back to an empty place of sadness. Finally, something had to break, he had to move forward and he had to get out of his apartment.

With his mind congested he decided to lace up his shoes and go for a run. Running had always been Brian's preferred form of escape. Running was a place where he could forget, a place where he did not have to think, a place where he could become lost in the cadence of his shoes striking the road or the trail surface in front of him. Most importantly today, running was a place where he could tune out.

The road felt good under his feet, Brian did not realize how much he needed the simple freedom running had to offer. His run time provided the opportunity to be himself again. His legs felt powerful, his lungs breathed comfortably and the effort it took to propel forward was easy. Lost in the comfort of the run, nothing bothered him. Life once again was perfect, nothing hurt, nothing felt empty and there were no concerns for tomorrow.

Just as he began to feel one with the open road and his mind became lost in the moment not preoccupied with tomorrow or yesterday the cadence of his foot strike became broken. Reality came crashing down on him as a passing car came a little too close. The startling noise was familiar and a little too near. The day he was trying desperately to set aside, if not to forget, came roaring back to the forefront of his consciousness.

The ensuing bolt of adrenaline caused Brian to haphazardly jump mid stride. As he sensed being airborne gravity won out causing an awkward landing on the side of the curb. His right ankle twisted a bit as the weight of his body landed on the road surface. Able to steady himself he came to a quick and abrupt stop. Instinctively he surveyed all his body parts to ensure everything was still intact and undamaged. Then he raised his arms high in the air as a sign of protest. He hoped that the driver would see him in his rearview mirror and understand that getting that close to a runner was not cool.

With the initial surprise and excitement over, his heart raced and his stomach turned. He knew it would be hard to get over his loss, he wasn't sure he wanted to get over it. "Man, it's not going to be easy getting used to that sound," Brian said to himself out loud and gasping for breath. He knew he never wanted to get over Abby. Brian wanted to hold on to every thought and memory he had of her. Catching his wits he once again pushed off and headed down the road, but this time instead of running aimlessly from one turn to another he had a purpose.

With nerves that were steadied once again, Brian knew he had to get used to the road noise that accompanied the majority of his training runs. It took the better part of a mile but as he approached a left-hand turn, a turn that was familiar to him, once again he was lost in the experience of the run.

Out of routine Brian made the turn and ran the fifty yards or so that would deliver him off the main road to a set of wrought iron gates. The gates stood at least 10 feet tall. Each wrought iron gate was impressive in its construction, ornamentation and spanned half the width of the double lane road leading up to a striking entrance.

The gates were shouldered by two red brick fences each one covered partially in moss. Numerous times Brian had run here before. The place was safe. The traffic if any was slow and respectful. Today his run inside the solemn gates would deliver him to Abby's grave site. This would be Brian's first visit since her funeral, 15 days earlier. He was not sure what he would find or how he would react, but something was calling him to this place.

Abby's grave sat along the back fence on a section of the cemetery that bordered a small forest. The atmosphere here was quiet, peaceful and perfect; if a grave site for a person so young could ever be perfect. Brian slowed his gait as he approached. His heart sank and his eyes grew damp as he caught a glimpse of the freshly sodded grass that appeared a little out of place. Walking the final paces that brought him to the edge of the road, his hands were on his hips, his lungs heaved as he was out of breath. Brian knew the final hundred feet from the road to graveside would be the longest distance he would ever have to travel.

His emotions raced and his mind questioned, was it too soon, was it too late. A lot of race finishes had been emotional for him, he broke down after his first 100-mile race, yet the final push to visit her grave had him

49

wondering if he could make it the final steps. Then something caught his attention as he looked toward the grave and it spurred him to move forward. Wiping the tears from his eyes he found that someone left a white teddy bear sitting among a collection of flowers. Brian wondered who left such a special gift. He remembered that the bear was not there when he left after the ceremony. He also noticed a gray flat rock about the size of a softball sitting out of place on the freshly laid sod. Held underneath the weight of this simple rock was a sheet of paper. It appeared that the paper had been there a few days as it was slightly weathered and crinkled.

As Brian reached the permanent site of her headstone, a cold chill came over him as he sat down and simply ran his finger through the grass. Catching his breath and gaining some composure, he reached out and picked up the rock sliding the note out from underneath it. Taking the note he noticed the handwriting. The letters were drawn out in a very feminine stroke, the words had a simple but elegant appearance to them, he reasoned it must have been written by a female. Wiping his eyes once again he began to read the letter.

Abby,
I miss you so much.

You were the one person who believed in me. When I went out for the cross-country team, I had no idea what I was doing or if I could even run the distances you inspired me to run. It's funny now, but I had no idea how long a mile was until I ran with you. You were a great coach, friend and someone I looked up to. Not sure if I ever told you, but you helped me feel comfortable in my own skin, in my own life. You made me feel proud of....me!

Thank you so much for running with us girls and with me. You were someone we could talk to, share our problems with and trust. I'll never forget you. I know there is a God, there has to be because he sent you, An Angel, to help me when I needed someone. I'm sorry you're gone but I'm happy knowing he has you with him.

Thank you, Abby

Beth

P.S. I never had a sister, but if I did I'm sure she would have been like you.

It was so touching reading the heartfelt thoughts written on that simple piece of paper. Brian knew how much the high school teams and the girls, Abby volunteer coached meant to her. Abby enjoyed spending time with the girls, she enjoyed being part of the team and she enjoyed giving back to her high school.

Brian sat at graveside and held a simple conversation. At times he did not know what he was saying and at other times he knew he was telling Abby how lost he was without her.

"Abby, I'm not sure I can do this. I'm not sure how to move on, I just want you back…I so miss you."

It was quiet in the cemetery. During the many times Brian ran the roads there he never noticed the complete stillness in the air until sitting next to Abby's grave. His heart was empty, his soul bare and yet he did not want to leave. Somehow being there made him feel closer to her. It felt good for him to be near her, to be near his Abby. The time passed quickly, the sun began to grow low in the sky. The chilling temperatures quickly made him feel cold. If he remained there much longer, he knew it would be a cold and dark run home. It was time to go back to the lonely apartment that now was no longer feeling like home.

It took a great amount of effort and determination for Brian to get up off the ground and to stand upright. If he had his choice, he would have stayed right there, next to Abby for the rest of his life. Brian knew he had to get back home, back to his life or what he had left of it.

Before beginning his lonely run home, Brian picked up the white teddy bear noticing someone put little doll sized running shoes on her feet and pinned a decorative rose to her chest. He was not sure why, but he knew he wanted to take this little bear with him. He hoped the person who put it there would understand.

The run home was quiet, just a heart broke young man and the sounds of his feet striking the ground. Brian did not think about much on the way home. He did not think about the funeral. He did not think about what he was going to do when he got home. He did not think about tomorrow, he only thought about the next step, the next stride, and the next foot strike. Five miles down the road Brian just wanted to get back to some sense of normal.

The next months after the accident, Brian tried to get back into a routine. He tried to regain his life. Abby's family invited him over for dinner, lunch, or a trip out of town. He enjoyed seeing them. But there was always that awkward pause, that painful moment where the conversation would turn to Abby. Or worse, how he was getting along without her. The more he tried to move on, the more he realized that most of his relationships were built around him and Abby being a couple. The town he planned to establish their life in stopped feeling like home. Everything seemed different after that terrible day.

In the community where he once felt a part of the group, he felt more like an outsider. Without Abby, he felt like the third wheel. He wondered if he was the tag-along guy. Everyone was sincere and caring. He knew it wasn't them; they wanted to include him. They felt for him. He lived with the burden of being "that" guy. He had become the guy that had a story. He felt more like an outsider, even as people were trying to comfort him.

Brian tried to fit in. He tried to adapt. For him, everything just felt out of place. The neighborhoods that Brian and Abby ran through, which might have been the location of their first home, now were constant reminders of what would not be. Their favorite trails now seemed foreign. The trails were once an escape for them to be alone. They shared a common bond; a common love for the outdoors. Now the familiar trails offered yet another lonely reminder of his loss.

Memories came alive on the trails and they stung at his heart. "We ran over there. I remember the time we stopped for a water stop here." Brian had tons of wonderful memories with Abby and he wanted to remember each and every one. Living them out over and over again in person, on location, just got to be too much. His world, which one day was perfect, had been turned upside-down and he needed a fresh start. Brian wanted to hold on to the memories but also was desperate to rid himself of the hurt.

There was one particularly dark and agonizing night that everything good felt like it had been removed from his life. The pain of separation weighed on him heavily. It got to be too much. It was during this miserable night that he was finally able to figure out a way to leave all the pain behind him. He began by writing two letters; one to Abby's parents and the other to the people whom he rented the apartment from. He did not want to leave any loose ends. Brian did not want to leave any pain or troubles for the people who had treated him like family.

A short distance across town a telephone rang and this caught Brian's mother off guard as it was late in the evening. "Hello mom, it's me." The course and despondent voice on the other end of the line startled her.

"Are you okay?" His mother instinctively replied. "What has happened?"

"I'm fine," He quickly tried to reassure her. Then he went on to explain his feelings. Brian and his mother were close; they had talked in the past in great depth about relationships, feelings, loss and love. They both shared some common wounds of failed relationships. He told her he could no longer live in the same apartment, the same neighborhoods or the same town as he had shared with Abby. He told her his hurt was too raw, that he had to get away to try and rebuild his life.

His mother understood. In a shaken voice she replied, "I don't want you to go, but that is for truly selfish reasons, you're my only son. I don't want you to leave, things will be alright." She paused, "But I also understand."

His mother further explained that she would worry about him. She also understood the great depths of his emotion. She told him she would always be there for him and that if he ever needed her, that she was a phone call away.

"I know Mom and I'm sorry. Abby was all I had…why did she have to leave. I've asked God and I just don't understand." His voice grew more broken. "Mom, I've shouted at God and been angry with him, why did she have to leave me? I've told him I don't understand."

They talked for over three hours; that was perhaps the longest phone conversation either one of them had ever had. She understood his resolve, reasoning, and motivation.

"Brian, I will miss you terribly. I'll always love you and will always support you." His mother replied.

"Thank you, Mom," Brian closed the conversation with a final statement, "I'm going to run Leadville, I'm not sure when but I'll find my way there." He took a deep breath, "Abby would have wanted me to run this race." He paused to catch his breath. "I love you, Mom, I'll be in touch." The phone line went silent.

The next morning, Brian was up before daybreak. Not taking long to shower and dress, he arranged his apartment in a neat and orderly fashion. He cooked himself a nice breakfast and tossed the remaining food items into the garbage. He then packed up his more personal items. After carrying the garbage bags to the dumpster, he made his way back to the apartment. Returning, Brian put together some boxes. He made a second trip, this time to the bed of his truck and once again returned inside. Grabbing a bottle of water, Brian sat on the couch and looked around the room. Scanning the four walls, his eye paused at a canvas picture of the Colorado Rockies. Although growing up all of his life within a stone's throw of Lake Erie, the great mountains of the West always called him. Brian could never explain but locations like Vail, Denver, and Colorado Springs always held his interest. His plan was to take Abby out west to the big mountains, as she called them, for their honeymoon.

He gave some more thought to his plan and with an ease of conscience he wrote out a check that would pay the remainder of his lease. On a separate piece of paper, he wrote out some instructions on what the owners could do with the remaining items inside his apartment. Then he looked at his watch. A GPS watch that would not only tell the correct time but also provide statistical data on his run. It was also a watch that Abby purchased for him. Staring at the digital face, it was time.

Brian took one last look around. A mini-highlight reel of all the good times he and Abby had shared together passed before his eyes. Brian walked to the door. He grabbed some items off the floor and turned off the lights. With one final pause, he pulled the door closed and locked it behind him. He slid the key under the door and gave it a final push. Brian knew it was time to move on.

Brian left the only place he had ever called home as an adult. This small town was the only world he had ever known. The two duffle bags and three boxes in the bed of his truck held everything that was important to him. Climbing into the cab of his truck, he settled himself behind the wheel, clicked the seat belt and took a deep breath. The empty seat next to him caught his attention. Brian's eyes fixed on it. He could not look away. Then his eye began to grow moist. His breathing changed. His chest grew tight, it felt like he could not breathe as the loneliness closed in. "Oh Abby, I miss you."

Sitting in his truck all alone Brian lost control of his emotions. The very raw feelings of sadness and anger could no longer be contained. Finally, after a few minutes, he was able to pull himself together. Brian was thankful no one was around to see him in such a state. With eyes, he could barely see out of he put the key in the ignition and started the engine. Wiping the tears from his eyes, he put the transmission into drive and eased out of the parking lot. He was heading to the main road that would lead to the freeway. The hurt felt familiar; he knew the pain of being alone. This time it was more intense, more real and deeper than anything Brian ever knew. He had one last action to take care of.

On the way out of town, Brian dropped the two letters into a street-corner mailbox. The first was addressed to his landlords. An older couple in their mid-50s' they were good people. They had always treated him fairly. He knew he was leaving them in a pinch and he wanted to make things right with them. The second was addressed to Abby's parents. This letter bared his soul and tried to explain why he was leaving town. He tried to explain why it hurt too much to live in the footsteps of a lost life. He tried to explain that he had to leave to be able to live without their Abby. He hoped the letter would explain how he felt and how much she meant to him.

The letter had taken him hours to write. Tormented by emotions and besieged by his own doubts it proved difficult to capture his true desires and meanings in simple words. By the time he was done, dozens of crumpled up white paper balls filled a small trash can while others laid wrinkled on his apartment floor. He agonized over every word, over every thought and feelings trying to explain. With all that effort he was still not sure he crafted all the words correctly. He had to explain to them why he was leaving town. He had to tell them why he could not see them in person. The letter also told them how much he loved Abby.

Inside that ordinary white envelope along with the letter and wrapped in white tissue paper was a ring. He hoped they would understand. He knew they felt his loss. He hoped he would see them again, someday. That someday would be when he felt whole again.

CHAPTER 6

A New Life

The distractions of establishing a new life in a new location kept some of the pain at bay. Although nothing removed the hurt or the loneliness that haunted him. Brian's new lifestyle paralleled that of a modern day gypsy. He would settle in a new town and begin to establish a new routine. Normally within six months to a year of setting up camp, he soon found that the surroundings began to creep in on him and things just did not feel right. After picking up and moving a few times he found that he felt most comfortable, that he was most settled emotionally when he was on the move. This unsettled nature and the emptiness in his heart sparked and fueled his running and his writing.

Running on an ever-changing landscape of park trails, roadways or mountain and canyon passes tied right into his rambling lifestyle. Without a permanent home address, Brian was able to select locations that kept him distracted while energizing his running and creative appetite. Brian enjoyed the excitement of visiting new locations, new trails, and running new races. He also experienced the town and the people in his temporary community like a local, but without the ties or responsibilities of being a resident.

Within the ultra running community, Brian found it easy to make friends. Runners in general and ultra runners as a whole are a different breed of people. The majority were accepting, humble and helpful when asked. Most kept to themselves or only associate within the select group of people with whom they share a bond. People outside of the community may see them as different. After all, who could understand why someone would want to run for five-plus hours if you had not experienced it yourself? Although Brian was able to tie into the local running communities and was accepted, he always felt on the fringe. The friendships he made were sincere but lacked the depth that only time provided. That was the downside of his lifestyle. He never stayed in one location long enough to develop a deep sustaining root system within the community.

This mobile living arrangement provided the opportunity to run and write about any location Brian chose. He would be running in the Blue Ridge Mountains for a few months, then move on for a race in the Badlands of South Dakota. Next, Brian would be part of a crew supporting a runner crossing Death Valley in the Legendary Badwater 135 mile ultra marathon.

Without a home base and not wanting to be subjected to the high costs associated with temporary apartments, Brian considered a number of different options before settling on one unique approach. Motivated by the desire to have some fashion of routine in his life. Brian purchased a truck camper that would be his home while he ventured about the country. Not one to go towards the lower end of the spectrum of anything he did, his was not a bare-bones canvas covered super-tent, but a top-of-the-line modern conveniently equipped recreational vehicle. Everything Brian needed and everything he cared about would be at his fingertips and within the confines of his mobile residence. The locations may change, but his home would be the same no matter where he ended up. Brian enjoyed that one little piece of consistency.

Explaining his accommodations to new friends was sometimes a challenge. Some people understood and appreciated the freedom it offered, while others looked at him in a way where he knew they questioned his intelligence. "Oh, you're a gypsy. No wait, a nomad", were the normal comments.

To try and explain, Brian would draw the comparison. "When you forget about the mobile nature, my home is really nothing more or less than a studio apartment, but on wheels." Some found this interesting, others a bit crazy. "The one big difference is, if I don't like my neighbors, I move," he often joked. This lifestyle provided everything a traditional stick and brick home offered and the versatility of being able to take everything with you.

To pay the bills, Brian continued his work as a contributor to *Trail Running & Beyond*. As the locations changed, the depth and breadth of his writings improved. Over time he gained a loyal following and the editors noticed. The editors understood his unique living situation. They also understood the pain of his loss. The chief editor and owner of the magazine felt it provided the momentum he needed as an author

Brian's writing success changed how he viewed a day on the trails. A run surrounded by the natural beauty of God's work was no longer miles in the log book leading up to the next race. Time on the trails or open roads was no longer attempts to shave a minute off his time or to increase his weekly mileage totals. Now running time became an extension of life with a meaningful experience. With a passion for telling a story as his blank canvas, it wasn't long before the editors noticed Brian's posts were some of the most popular features in their magazine. With all of his mounting success, the editor offered Brian a full-time position. Brian's new title would be Chief Running Contributor. This position gave him the ability to go on assignment covering any running related event he desired. With the freedom of flying solo, Brian took advantage of the opportunity.

Eventually though, Brian found himself growing lonely. The only true companion he had while out on the road was the white teddy bear. His overstuffed and forever smiling travel companion sat in a special spot under the TV on the corner of the cabinet space between the kitchenette and the over the cab bed.

It was a cool fall night while out shopping for some cooking supplies. Brian was drawn into an establishment, the type of which he had not frequented for years. He was unsure why he entered, but it was a day that changed the lives of two kindred spirits. He met a girl. She was fun, spirited and had a calming effect on his soul. She noticed him first and was determined to seize his attention. As most girls do who are looking for a friend in such a place, she acted in a flirtatious way as to surely draw his attention. Their eyes met. Brian was instantly attracted to her. His heart melted. She made him feel wanted again. She knew she had him; her brown eyes simply pulled him in deeper. Caught in her spell, he simply stared at her. From that moment, Brian knew he had never seen such a beautiful dog.

At first, Brian just wanted to play with the puppy who caught his attention. He thought he would kill some time during a lonely night, no sense going back to the camper so soon. Maybe he could toss a ball around or play a game of keep away. He asked the store manager if he could hold the little girl. The manager jumped at this opportunity and fetched the puppy out of her kennel. Within seconds of being placed in Brian's arms, there was a bond between the two of them. The little puppy looked kind of scared and unsure. Brian held her up close to his face and whispered, "It's okay, girl, I'm a friend." The puppy must have felt the warmth in his voice. She rolled her head onto his chest right above his heart. The top of her head rested right under his chin, Brian loved the puppy smell. He cuddled her up and patted her on her head.

Brian knew their lives were now connected. He could not stomach the idea of this wonderful little girl going back into the cold kennel all alone. He also had enough lonely nights entertaining himself. He figured the two of them might as well keep each other company. Brian adopted the salt-and-pepper six-month-old Miniature Schnauzer on the spot. When it came time to fill out the paperwork, he named her Hanna Lizbeth. From that day forward, other than when he was out running, they were always together. Brian would need the companionship, as it was time to move again. And this time, a major challenge lay in waiting.

Although Brian had enjoyed his time in the Ohio Valley he reached that point where he felt the call to a new adventure. As he broke down camp, instead of randomly selecting the next location to visit, Brian knew in advance where the road would take him this time. With his new role of Chief Running Contributor, his next feature would encompass one of the hardest personal challenges he had ever faced. Brian's next adventure would be the Leadville Trail 100, a 100-mile mountain endurance race also known as the "Race Across the Sky."

CHAPTER 7

Moving to Leadville

Leadville is a historic mountain town nestled among the highest mountain peaks in Colorado. Surrounded by a high alpine forest, with mountain streams and lakes formed by glaciers, Leadville has a unique atmosphere. It's home to some wonderful trails retracing its glory days as a mining town. It's also a small town with all the feel and charm of days gone by. The population has gradually decreased from 14,000 during the silver/gold boom of the 1900s to the nearly 3,000 that call Leadville home today. Leadville is also home to a world famous foot race.

The legendary Leadville Trail 100, aka the "Race Across The Sky", is a mountain trail race run over one hundred miles, reaching extreme elevations in the Colorado Rockies. An out-and-back course, it travels mostly on forest trails and mountain roads. Runners conquer places like Twin Lakes and Hope Pass, at a staggering 12,600 feet above sea level. This is a race where you give your all, you hope to finish and some hope to survive. This is also a race that changes people. A few run Leadville to win. Many run Leadville hoping to gain respect for the mountain and earn respect from the running community. In some cases, some run Leadville to settle a broken soul.

Brian once heard someone describe climbing Hope Pass as "running straight up and into the sky." Since that day, the race had always garnered his attention. The high starting elevation, 10,200 feet and the changes in elevations along the way offered a major challenge that fueled his strong desire to prove his worth. The struggles inherent in covering 100 miles in such conditions were many. Like a fish that took the bait, Brian was hooked.

The obvious challenges were the mountains; towering into the sky they dominate the landscape. The Colorado Rockies are ancient rock formations that were shifted from their then horizontal position, lifted up and pressed vertically into the sky. The 100-mile course starts in the center of Leadville, Colorado. This little hamlet of a town is the highest incorporated city in the U.S., sitting at 10,000 feet above sea level where the oxygen is very thin. The race course takes runners 50 miles out to the old ghost town of Winfield, Colorado and then 50 miles back.

Brian had successfully run his share of mountain races before. He'd run a number of 100-milers but he had never run anything like this. Over the past year, he'd built a race calendar and training plan designed to prepare himself for the extreme challenge Leadville offered. He had logged nearly 800 miles in the Blue Ridge Mountains preparing himself. Everything he had learned from past finishers indicated that it was best to get out to the mountains as early as you could. This helped your adjustment to the altitude. Since Brian had no real obligation keeping him tied down, he decided to head out to Colorado four months prior to race day.

This would be Brian's first trip to Leadville. Along with the adjustment period for the elevation change, Brian mapped out a training plan that had him running "the Silver Rush." This 50-mile race was the little sister event that run in mid-June. The shorter race was an exciting draw for him, but finding out what life in the high mountains was all about, was his real secondary goal. Brian's aim was not to simply add the Leadville

Trail 100 on his running resume. He was not simply interested in earning a Leadville Buckle, he was fascinated with its history, culture and the lore the race held over runners who came from all over the world to run it. Not confining his pre-race preparation solely on how to run Leadville, Brian immersed himself in the Leadville lifestyle.

Prior to breaking down camp, Brian researched what living life in Leadville was all about. From his internet information windfall, he selected a campsite with the closest access to the trails and a short distance from town. Brian would be staying at Sugar Loafin Campground. This location would be right along the opening section of the course where the runners headed out to Turquoise Lake and the May Queen Aid Station 13 miles into the race. He also gathered information on the local running scene. Brian had previously met a few Leadville finishers at other events. These relationships provided a few connections once he arrived in town. Leadville was going to be more than a race.

The drive to Leadville was uneventful. Hanna slept the majority of the trip while hogging much of the front seat. Brian focused on driving his home-on-wheels occasionally daydreaming about the race. His mind also drifted off to the time he told Abby about his dream to run the big three mountain trail races. Western States 100, Leadville Trail 100 and Hardrock 100 are the crown jewels of the ultra running community within the United States. It was exciting for him to think about accomplishing such an endurance test. It also pained him to remember that conversation with Abby. Everyone else with whom he shared his dream chuckled while others outright laughed at his dream. Some thought he was nuts. It especially hurt when he told his father. His father, although never attending his races or getting involved for much of his life, advised him he should not attempt such a thing. That it was "crazy" for him to even consider he could attempt such an arduous challenge. In contrast, Abby encouraged and believed in him.

Arriving in Leadville, Brian found comfort knowing that this would be his home-town for a longer period of time. This extended time in Colorado not only allowed him to train at altitude but also allowed him to mingle with the local running community. One thing that was easy for Brian was that he fit in well with people of similar interests. Outwardly, people may have said he was shy; once connected on a common thread, conversations become easy. He was very transparent about his lifestyle and the events that had brought him to this point in his life. Brian generally enjoyed being around people cut from the same fabric of life. With his home front settled, Brian and Hanna sensed a peaceful, accepting feeling over life in their new home.

On the rare occasion that Brian set his alarm, the not-so-pleasant buzzer went off at five a.m. This was a special day. Hanna was not so sure. She gave her human buddy a look that best can be described as timidly awake. When Brian got up and rattled around in the camper, somehow she knew it was time to start her day. After pulling on a black pair of shorts and a light weight green shirt, he grabbed a quick bite to eat. Done with breakfast, Brian filled his water bottle and grabbed his GPS watch. Hanna now up and moving bounced around the camper as Brian pulled on his favorite trail shoes. Hanna was now awake and eager to get outside and get her morning routine started. For her, it was just another new day at a new location. For her human counterpart, it was going to be his first run in Leadville. His first run at altitude and he was well aware that this run was going to hurt. Before venturing out on the trails Brian enjoyed his time tending to his little fur girl. In such a short time, she had really captured his heart the last few months.

Taking Hanna out for her morning stroll around the campsite, Brian noticed a sense of inner joy and happiness. He was also a touch anxious. After all the chores of setting up camp were complete, it was finally the day to stretch out his legs. Hanna, the ever-excited puppy, was happy to be outside. As much as Brian enjoyed running down a trail, she loved walking aimlessly around camp. One minute she was busy investigating the stack of firewood, the next she found the trail of a visiting squirrel who came by looking for leftover peanuts from a late night around the campfire. It was natural for her nose to lead the way. Brian always kept a watchful eye on her to make sure she did not venture far from his side or their site. Truth be told, he could watch her go from one interesting smell to another all day long. Once Hanna's morning routines were taken care of, Brian placed her back into the camper. Leaning into the doorway he gave her a pat on the head and a kiss on the muzzle. "I'll be back, little' girl…you be good." Locking the door to the camper, Brian headed out of the campground, his route pointed to the trails.

At a slow and easy pace, he made his way to the trail head. Once at the beginning of the trail leading to and around Turquoise Lake, Brian stopped. Staring up at the bright sky, he took a deep breath that filled his lungs to maximum capacity with crisp rocky mountain air. Meanwhile, out of habit, he raised one foot onto his toes then rolled his ankles around in little circles. It was a move he picked up from Abby and carried on out of routine. Once feeling all limbered up and ready to take on this first outing, Brian just stood still and was quiet for a few moments. Then, before pushing off, he paused. With closed eyes, the sun beaming down on his face, Brian offered up a simple prayer. "Thank you, Lord, for all these blessings…" At the very end of his prayer, "This is for you, Abby, I love you and I miss you so much." One tear formed neatly in the corner of his eyes and nearly rolled down his cheek as his right foot pushed him forward and onto the trail.

That first run and the weeks that followed establish a pattern that soon had his legs and lungs in top shape. Brian's weekly mileage was soon upward of seventy to eighty miles per week. The first few weeks also connected him with some new friends, a couple old acquaintances and a comfortable way of life. His routine had evolved to include morning runs on Monday, Wednesday, and Friday. Tuesday and Thursday, Brian would head out for some evening training runs after the sun went down. Running at night was very much a part of a successful run at Leadville. Saturday was for long runs hovering around 20 to 35 miles. Sunday was a day of worship and rest.

Apart from his training, Brian's time was filled with working around his camp, working on a novel, or drafting a column for *Trail Running & Beyond.* What Brian liked most, aside from running, was entertaining Hanna. She was really a smart dog besides being a really good friend. Brian initially worried about how she would adjust to his mobile nature.

It did not take her long to get accustomed to the roaming camper lifestyle. He soon found out she picked up on his commands very fast. With Brian's near-full attention it was not long before Hanna mastered all the typical dog obedience commands.

Hanna filled in for much of the emptiness in Brian's life; she offered him a warm welcome home after a run and a patient ear when he needed it. She was always an attentive listener to his training plans, feature magazine ideas or goals for his life, except when she fell asleep, as was often the case. Hanna was his sole dinner companion most nights. That arrangement worked well for the both of them. Hanna gave love and companionship and in return, she always had a full bowl of food and water, a partner for long walks, playtime and someone to trust. Most importantly, they both gained someone to love. She was always there for him in his loneliest moments and Brian offered her security and love. Even though they were content in each other's company, it was a good night when someone came calling.

On a few occasions, some of the local runners Brian met ventured out to his camp. They came for various reasons. Most stopped by to check out the new guy who may be competing in a race. Some came out to see what the guy who lives in his truck camper was really all about. Some, who had uncovered his day job, came to visit a small-time notable in the running world. Brian's lifestyle was out of the ordinary for most, but those that ventured out to get to know him, departed knowing Brian was a simple guy. He was a guy who was also a talented runner. Brian was a guy who had been handed a slightly different course in life than most.

CHAPTER 8

Meeting Michele

The time came when Brian was set to tackle one of the monster climbs on the Leadville Trail course. As the morning sunshine began to break through the camper windows, Brian stirred from a peaceful sleep. Coming to his senses, he wondered why he was given the gift of being an early riser. He did not ponder this question long nor did it take long for him to get moving. His four-legged companion, not an early riser by nature, took a little more coaxing. At first, Hanna jumped at his initial movements and then stuck her face back into the blanket that was bunched up at Brian's feet.

Hanna went back to sleep. One trait Brian found amusing about his little puppy was that at just the sheer mention of the words "go to bed" Hanna was off. The little dog broke all land-speed records pulling off acrobatic moves that would make the finest Olympic gymnasts proud as she raced off to bed. A benefit to beginning able to out run her best friend was that she normally selected the prime spot and was out cold before her master could turn off the lights. Today was a new day. Brian was going to take on a new challenge and it was time to get moving.

Up and about Brian washed his face and fixed his shortly trimmed but wavy hair. Staring into the bathroom mirror, his blue eyes looked right back, "Well today is the first of the big training runs, no backing out." Hanna barked at him as he spoke to himself, she was finally ready to greet the world and that meant she was ready to go outside.

The forecast for the day was mild temperatures with bright, clear skies. Ruffling through his running gear, Brian pulled out a light short-sleeved shirt and shorts. "Come on, girl, time to get up and go out," he called out to his faithful companion. With those familiar words, Hanna stood on all four paws then stretched by pushing her face back into the blankets as her doggie butt went up in the air. Then, once all her little bones were limbered up, she jumped down from the over the cab bed and onto the dinette sofa. Her next landing spot was on the floor. After a full body, fur ruffling shake, Hanna headed towards the door. It was official: Hanna was ready to start her day.

Once the door was open, Brian glanced up at the mountains that surrounded Leadville, marveling at the thin clouds holding on to the peaks that towered into the heavens. A bright blue sky greeted this beautiful Saturday morning. It was on a morning much like this when Brian lost Abby.

It was on mornings like this that his heart felt the most vacate. It had been hard for him to get over the loss. Life moves on and he had adjusted, but this loss was always near the surface. Brian worked hard to improve his work, to become a better writer, likewise, he became more serious about his running. He also worked hard to regain touch with the world and meet new people. There had been opportunities for friendship and maybe more with a few girls. Some may have had the potential for romance. Brian always kept these women at a self-imposed distance. He never really opened up, he never really allowed his heart to be exposed. To Brian, it just never felt right.

Gingerly carrying Hanna down the stairs, he placed his favorite fur-ball

on the ground and they headed out on their walk. While walking Brian
sipped on his morning pick-me-up, a Diet Dew and munched on a Cliff
bar. Hanna had her nose to the ground and was busy sniffing all the fresh
smells of a new day. "Hanna, today is a long-run day and when I get
back, you and I will walk into town." Hanna's short-cropped tail flicked
side to side and one ear perked up. Brian was never sure if she
understood exactly what he said. One thing Hanna knew, that by the tone
of Brian's voice it was going to be fun and that made her happy.

At the end of their walk, Brian lifted Hanna up to put her back inside
the camper. He paused at the doorway to give her a big morning hug,
ruffling her up with a scratch behind the ears. "Hanna dog, it sure is great
having you in my life…you're my favorite fur-face." With that, he
placed her back inside the doorway and gave her one last pat on her
head. "I'll be right back, girl." Brian then closed and locked the door.

Today's run was a planned out-and-back route that covered the trail
around Turquoise Lake. This route passed the first of the Aid Stations at
May Queen and out to the Aid Station location at Fish Hatchery. This
route covered the first of the bigger climbs of the race and provide nearly
3,000 feet of elevation change. Brian knew he was in for a good workout.
This would be the first major test of his ability in the thin mountain air.
The plan for the day was to run this trail pretty hard. He would run the
outbound leg of the trail up and over Sugarloaf Pass, to Fish Hatchery.
There he would hit some water and food and turn around running it all
over again. Today would provide not only a solid workout but also a test
drive of the running vest backpack setup he planned to use during the
race. The one thing Brian wanted today on his first big climb since
arriving at Leadville was no surprises.

From the campground to the trailhead, Brian ran at a moderate pace.
The first mile out on the trail felt light and easy. His feet barely felt like
they were coming into contact with the ground as he moved along.
Rounding up one turn and into another, everything was clicking along
like a well-oiled timepiece. His legs felt powerful. His feet landed firmly
on the ground. The push off into the next stride was perfect. Not only

were his legs performing at top level but breathing came easy today. Days before, he'd sounded like an old worn-out freight train, puffing his way around town. Much improved, today he breathed as if he was performing at sea level. The only caution of the day was the trail surface. Brian knew that he needed to keep his attention and vision lowered on the ground in front of him to avoid a wrong step or worse, a twisted or broken ankle.

Midway through the run, life on the trail was feeling very good. Brian had summited Sugarloaf Pass and was making his way to Fish Hatchery. Here he stopped quickly to catch his breath, swap out his water bottles, grab an energy gel while getting ready to bound back up the trail. But before he could push off something caught his eye.

Overhead a bald eagle was flying majestically surveying the ground, looking for his next meal. Out of a convenient pocket on the front of his running vest, Brian broke out a small digital camera. It only took a few seconds to snap a collection of pictures that would last a lifetime. Brian loved trail running, being well aware that most of nature's beauty was off the beaten path. He wanted to run and run fast, but you had to take the time to take in the experience, the sights, and the grandeur. The camera was tucked back in his vest and within seconds he pushed off, making his way back up the climb. Half his training run the first real climb since coming to Leadville was done. Now he just needed to seal the deal and come away without tearing up anything, mainly himself.

Going downhill to an ordinary runner always sounded easy compared to running up a hill. For a mountain runner who may be subjected to hours of downhill, the intense hammering on the quads could end the day just as fast as anything else. The Leadville course offered hours of downhill, which could trash the thighs. Many a strong runner had been cast along the side of the trail with legs unable to continue moving forward as a result of this downhill assault. Come race day, the real challenge may not be getting up Hope Pass, it may just be coming back down twice and there is no fast fix for that.

The positive side of downhill running is that you can cover ground really fast. The bad side of running downhill is that everything happens very quickly. A wrong foot placement could end your day in rapid, and violently fashion. A moment out of balance or a foot catching on a rock and you could come crashing into the trail superman-style, normally flying head first into any number of sharp, jagged or protruding objects. Everything happens faster on the downhill, a twisted ankle, a bruised foot or it could be worse. Nearly done with his first big test Brian wanted to finish up and avoid all of that drama.

At the halfway point down the mountain, Brian's leg turnover, foot placements, and gravity were all in tune. He was covering ground at a good clip. Settled into an easy to maintain cadence, he was able to keep up a reasonably fast pace. To run the downhill sections fast, the runner not only had to keep an eye on their foot placement but also look through the turns into the next leg of the downhill. It was during one of these switchbacks that something flashed into his line of sight. It happened so fast, there was no time to adjust his course. The only thing that was certain was that the oncoming object and he were on an intersecting path and it was too late to do anything but brace for impact.

Another runner approaching from the opposite direction collided with him in the center of a blind turn. After the initial impact Brian still on his feet, but staggering, tried desperately to regain his balance. When his eyes were finally able to see who he made contact with he realized it was a girl. He tried to reach out to her but he was tumbling in the opposite directions and she was just out of arm's length. Within seconds their momentum deposited them into a heap of twisted bodies lying on the ground amongst a small cloud of dust and dirt.

"Oh, I'm so sorry," Brian reacted naturally. "Are you okay?"

The girl lifted her head from the dirt trail. "Me? What? Are you okay? I wasn't looking where I was going and you're bleeding."

"What, I'm bleeding?" With a slight hint of panic in his voice, Brian glanced down at his leg, checking out a scratch on the back of his right thigh. It did not take him long to figure out it was superficial. "Oh that, it's nothing. Seriously, are YOU okay?"

"I'm fine," she replied, then burst out laughing. "Oh, we have to look like a bunch of buffoons…the entire Rocky Mountains to run in, not another soul out here and we run into each other. This will be one of those stories."

After sharing a laugh and picking themselves up, Brian said, "I won't tell…if you don't."

"If you do tell this story to your running buddies, at least tell them I was being chased by a bear, mountain goat or at least a crazed squirrel, make it sound heroic." she said in a soft, feminine yet secure tone.

Michele was a Leadville transplant, although many in the community considered her a local. She moved to Leadville five years ago, coming off a divorce from her former husband. He was an abusive guy. Michele was spirited, outgoing and welcoming to new friendships, but slow to really engage. She was a naturally beautiful girl, not one of the manufactured and Hollywood-processed beauties. Michele's personality captured any room she walked into. Today she grabbed ahold of Brian's attention.

After the shock of the collision and assessment that all body parts were still functioning, Brian did something completely out of character.

"I'm so sorry, are you sure you are okay?" He paused for a moment as if gaining strength and catching his breath. "Would you like to meet up sometime? We could grab a snack, dinner or coffee."

Michele, brushing dirt and dried leaves off of her shirt and hair, replied "Yea I'm okay. I'm just dusty. I'm Michele, by the way." A slight pause followed. "With one L. Since you almost took me out, if you're buying, I'm eating."

"Oh, yea might as well get the formal introductions out of the way. I'm Brian, with one" he paused for a quick second, "With one B, yeah that's it." They both chuckled a little and made plans to meet up later that evening at a little diner in town.

As fast as it all transpired, they were both secure on their feet again and busy dusting off the trail dirt, small rocks, and dead foliage. There was an awkward pause. Michele broke the silence first. She smiled. "I'll see you later, right?" She turned and ran out on the trail again.

Brian stood there watching as she disappeared. "What just happened?" He wondered in silence. It took him a few moments to take it all in and to regain his composure. Continuing with this internal dialogue, he thought, "I'm not sure if I should be upset because this girl messed up my training run or happy because I don't have to eat alone tonight." Brian paused, then answered himself, this time out loud. "I'm going to be happy. I have a companion for dinner."

He finished brushing all the dirt and debris off his shorts then dealt with the blood running down his leg. All of this time off his feet did not cause much of a delay. With Michele out of sight, it was time to get back to work. Brian pushed off with his right foot to restart his run and his trek downhill. With the extra surge of adrenaline, it did not take him long to reach the end of the trail. Once off the trail, he stopped to catch his breath. His heart was pounding in his chest, he wanted to try and figure out just what happened up on the trail. "A dinner date with a girl? With a girl, I just met, ran into, and was nearly killed bye?" Of all the things Brian had thought could happen on the trail today, this was not one of them.

Brian returned to the campground and to his site. The sound of his footfall penetrated the thin walls of his mobile studio apartment and caught the attention of a stirring miniature schnauzer. Hanna's more dominating ear perked up, then the other followed suit. Once she recognized the familiar sound of her traveling companion returning home, her head popped off the pillow and she jumped up on all fours, wide awake and eager to see him.

After a slight cool-down walk Brian rounded the back of his campsite, approached the stairs that led to the camper door. After stopping for a brief second to wipe the sweat off his forehead and to take the last drink from his water bottle, he slid the key into the lock and opened the door. With the door swinging open he got a clear view inside. The door was not open even a half a second before a bright and cheerful puppy face popped into view.

With half her tongue hanging out of her mouth, Hanna was a ball of energy at the sight of her very best friend. "Hi there, girl, told you I would be back,"

Hanna's cropped tail was in overdrive wagging back and forth; the momentum caused her little butt to shift side to side. Her entire world had come back to spend time with her and she was as happy to greet him as he was to see her. Seeing Hanna when he returned from a run or a day shopping was always welcomed. Her little face, puppy eyes and trademark schnauzer beard brightened up even the worst days and provided companionship during the lonely nights. Brian's first order of business was to pick up his little girl, give her a big hug then they took off together on a walk. After their stroll, he'd get to a proper clean-up and put on some fresh clothes. Brian was still surprised at the events of the day. He left expecting a shakedown run in the mountains and came back with plans for dinner that did not involve meals out of a box, pizza or TV dinners. "Hey Hanna, you would never guess what happened today."

Just as he had not seen Michele on the trail, Brian had not seen this coming. His life had been full of confusion, rejection, and loneliness after losing Abby. After that terrible day, he never thought he would find love again. At times after her death, he wasn't even sure he wanted to. It had been a few years but his heart was still tender, his emotion still fragile and his love still protected. Besides all of this he knew he wanted to learn more about the girl who ran him over on the trail. He wanted to see her again. He could not explain it but from almost the first time he looked into her eyes after they came to a rest on the ground, something drew him in. Something about Michele caught his attention.

When Brian talked with Hanna she would stop whatever she was doing, look up at him and tilt her head. Brian enjoyed the connection. Up to this point, his world had been very narrow in focus and she was often on the other end of many conversations. "I really have no idea why I asked her to have something to eat with me." Brian was very cautious to not use the word, date. " I wasn't really looking for anything, I just wanted to spend more time with her. You think that will be okay?" After a pause in the conversation, Hanna went back to walking and finding new smells to investigate.

CHAPTER 9

Michele's Story

"With one B, ha, that's cute." Michele laughed, then finished dusting herself off. Adjusting her running gear she confirmed the plans for dinner later that evening and then turned to continue on her way. As she disappeared along the trail Brian noticed how easily she accelerated and how gracefully she moved. Still caught off-guard at what had just transpired he stood there motionless as Michele departed the scene of the trail-running crime.

Michele was a fit and active girl, twenty-six years old with slightly longer than shoulder-length blonde hair and hazel eyes. Her long, tan legs made quick work out of a fluid running stride. Her appearance equaled that of any swimsuit, or fitness model featured on the covers of the latest get fit magazines. She was a true American beauty in every sense of the word. Her smile would stop the conversation in any room she entered and was what Brian remembered as he turned his attention back to the trail. "Man, what just happened?" he said to himself. "I'm running along, minding my own business, and wham I nearly get killed and now I have a dinner date. Who was that girl?"

Brian continued on his way replaying every detail of what he could remember of the encounter. For a second he was more lost in his thoughts about Michele than alert on the trail. Next thing he knew, his toe caught on a root and he nearly found himself in the dirt again.

Growing up, Michele was the second of four children, two boys, and two girls. The first girl of a mainly Catholic family, she was the apple of her daddy's eye. Her formative years were spent within the dynamics of a large family. Nearly all her relatives, there were a lot of them, lived within ten miles of her home in small-town Minnesota. Her family was close. Most weekends they spent at picnics, church bazaars or fishing on one of the nearby lakes. She enjoyed spending time fishing with her father. Michele loved eating freshly caught fish. Everyone in Minnesota, the land of 10,000 lakes, enjoyed fishing. She grew up a bit of a tomboy, but inside was all sugar and spice and everything nice. She hated bugs, worms, and cleaning fish. She especially hated baiting the hooks. She loved being active and treasured the time with her family.

In high school, despite knowing almost everyone in her class, Michele felt out of place. Although popular and outgoing, she did not get to attend all the functions, nor participate in most sports or social gatherings. On many a Friday night, while her friends were at the football game she was at home. It was common for her to miss out on the open skating time at the local rink. With a large family, there just was not enough time and money to get everyone to every event. Falling into that traditional middle-child role, she missed out on a lot of activities she wanted to participate in. She often dreamed of the day when she could follow her own ambitions. She daydreamed of being self-sufficient and she fantasized, like any young girl, of finding true love. Still, Michele grew up happy and content.

Michele graduated from high school, not at the top of her class and not at the bottom either. She was bright and intelligent, but never found her niche with her studies. She worked a few odd jobs around town but eventually grew tired of smelling like tacos and earning minimum-wage.

She wanted more out of herself and her life. That sense of wanting something more from the world led her to enlist in the United States Air Force. She considered the Marines for a short time but eventually headed south for Air Force Basic Training. Within a year of graduating high school, Michele sat in coach headed to Lackland Air Force Base, San Antonio, Texas, the world and her future looked bright.

Military life came easy for her. Her life had settled into an easy routine. Michele made friends fast. Her first duty assignment in the northern tier was Grand Forks Air Force Base, North Dakota. She also made a first-class impression while on-duty. She was proficient at her work and quick to pick up new tasks or learn new skills. Off-duty, with a stable income she was independent enough to be able to do what she wanted to do. With her own living accommodations and transportation, she was able to be active on base. Michele played softball on the base team. She was also an involved member of many enlisted and military councils.

With a wider social network than was available in her hometown, she met a lot of interesting people from all over the United States and in some cases from other parts of the world. Then, the next thing she knew, she met a boy. Things progressed fast. Before she had time to catch her breath they were married. During her tour at Grand Forks, Uncle Sam and the Department of the Air Force said they needed her services elsewhere. She enjoyed living away from home but close enough to go home and visit once in a while. Michele was a bit startled when she received orders that her next assignment would be on a little island in the Pacific called Guam.

As a young sergeant, Michele fit in well. Her professional presence in her unit made her an asset from day one. She was smart, efficient and made quick progress through the Air Force enlisted rank structure. Her career field was as a paralegal. She enjoyed her time at work. She felt challenged and stimulated with her duties; a far cry from stuffing and wrapping tacos. Her main tasks included preparing legal papers, reviewing case files and occasionally seeing the system work for the good guys. When she wasn't on duty Michele enjoy hanging out on the beach and playing softball. Success followed her there as well. She was selected for the base all-star team. This honor provided her the opportunity to travel around the Pacific. During her time at Anderson Air Force base, Guam, Michele blossomed into an independent young woman.

Her marriage started off shaky nearly from the honeymoon and maybe even before. There were cracks in the foundation and Michele knew it. The longer they were married, the more concerned she became that their union may have been a convenient way for her husband to break away from his former life. With a ring on Michele's finger, her husband paid very little attention to her. He spent his time socializing with new friends and playing golf. Instead of being at home with an attractive young wife, he was in the bars and hanging out at the golf course. Inside, Michele thought maybe she had done something wrong.

There were some good days, but they became less frequent. Michele's carefree life, a life she had been dreaming about since being a young girl, came crashing down one night. After all was said and done, she couldn't even remember what the argument was about. What she could remember was he hit her, she woke up on the living room floor and there was a terrible pain on the right side of her face.

Mr. Right became cold and mean. Then he became more abusive. Although he said he was sorry, and that it wouldn't happen again, it did and soon became routine. At first, she blamed the marks, the bruises on her clumsiness but soon people noticed and asked questions. Then she could no longer hide it from her co-workers. Some reached out, others just talked under their collective breath. She was scared. Michele went from feeling successful and proud to shameful and feeling like a failure.

Confused and alone, Michele didn't know what to do. One dark night while she sat alone in an empty house she picked up the phone and dialed the familiar phone number. Thousands of miles away, the message got lost in translation or distance. It may have been that she was scared to tell her family everything. The true message may not have been clearly communicated. Up to this point, Michele had only shared with them the good news, the happy times. The image she reported back home was that of a happy life. They thought she had met her prince charming and was living the happily ever after part of the fairy tale endings.

Her parents were shocked. The facade was down and the untold life of abuse was found out. Her parents were upset and confused. Michele broke down; this was the first time she had admitted failure to her father.

The news hit hard. Her father was upset. He offered to come out and help. Her family was angry and bitter but unsure of what to do themselves. The only advice they offered did very little to provide comfort or direction: "We have never had a divorce in the family, try your best to work it out." As the line went dead and she hung up the phone, Michele felt isolated and alone.

Trusting her parents' advice, she tried to work it out. Michele attempted to get into a marriage counseling program. She thought for sure that with some professional help they would get on a better path. Her husband wanted nothing of that idea. Counseling was rejected flat-out. Michele tried her hardest to be better, to be the perfect wife. Months went by and at times there seemed to be a glimmer of hope. Then something would set him off and each time he got worse. She could no longer hide the marks, the shame or the fear.

More people at work noticed. Her friends noticed the marks became larger, deeper and appeared more often. Lost in the middle of it all, Michele was not sure what to do. Then, after one severely brutal incident where she feared for her life, she finally reached her tipping point, she finally had enough. She decided this had to end. Michele summoned all of her strength, all of her resolve, and told him he was moving out. Today. For good.

A divorce came fast. He did not contest the proceeding or anything in the decree. Michele cited irreconcilable differences as the grounds. It took just a few weeks for the legal process to work. The next thing Michele knew it was time to appear in front of a judge.

The judge asked a few simple questions, "Can this marriage be saved?

Are their children? Have you worked out the resolution of the debts and finances?"

It was easy for Michele to respond with all the correct and anticipated answers. She truly wanted out of this disaster of a relationship. Her soon-to-be-ex-husband just stood there; he agreed to all the terms. Then the judge paused and asked, "Was there any violence in the marriage?"

The judge's words hung in the air. Michele's eyes diverted from the judge and looked down to the nearly healed bruise on her right wrist. The brownish mark with a hue of purple reminded her of their last altercation. The night he pushed her to the ground and grabbed something off the kitchen counter. She remembered the blunt force of the impact and nearly blacking out.

The sting of the question hit at Michele's soul. Its impact made her feel like a wounded little girl. She never thought she would be in this position. She wanted to open up and tell the judge and the world everything. Michele stood there in silence, she kept quiet.

For the price of silence, she could be done with this period of her life. She could be done with him. Mostly she could be done with it all. She remained quiet. Her eyes shifted and focused on the pattern of the highly polished floor tiles. She held her breath and replied, "No, sir." Michele's voice cracked as she attempted to get the words out. The judge saw a tear run down her cheek. With all of his years of experience, the judge translated that short reply into a true testament of the soon to be dissolved marriage.

With a swift motion, the gavel made its impact with the bench and a louder than normal thud echoed in the court-house. The Honorable Judge Emerson dissolved the marriage with one parting comment. "Son, don't you let me see you in here again." Hearing the finality of the judge's comments, Michele wiped her cheek. Taking a deep breath she held her head high, turned around and walked out a free woman.

As fate would have it, the termination of her marriage occurred during the same time when Michele's enlistment was up. Deciding whether to continue her career or to return to the civilian sector was a hard decision.

She loved the military life. She felt valued in the skills she provided her country. It weighed on her constantly. It was not an easy choice. Finally, after much turmoil, she decided it was time to get out of the military. Michele figured she needed a complete change in atmosphere.

The news was hard to deliver to her supervisor. He asked her to not do anything serious until she spoke with the commander. Within hours the squadron commander, a very busy man with a lot of responsibilities cleared his calendar. Lt Col Green called her into his office. He first wanted to say how sorry he was, that he had no idea this was happening under his watch. "As a man, I'm appalled, as a father I'm upset and as your Commander, I want to do whatever is best for you. But I also don't want to see you lose a career over this." He paused to gain his composure, "frankly over this loser, of a man." He wanted to comfort her and also offer some reasoning.

"Michele, I am sorry what happened to you at home. But don't let that bad experience cost you a wonderful career." He told her, "You have so much to offer your country and the Air Force. Your skills, drive and professionalism will take you far." Despite his best intentions, she wanted to leave the bad memories behind her. She wanted to start fresh and to be new again. Michele confirmed that she'd decided to move on.

As part of the separation package, the Air Force would transition those "Honorably Discharged" to their home of record. The member could also select any place of their choosing, as long as it was closer to their last assigned base.

Michele made many close friends while on Guam. As the assignment season came, many of them were moving on to their next duty stations as well. She considered moving to North Dakota; good friends Jon and Rhonda were moving there. Then she considered Georgia, where Kendra and Jeff started a family. She reasoned she had a lot of options. So many, in fact, that it almost became too much to consider. Michele spent many hours trying to figure out her next move. The military assignment systems gave her 30 days to make her selection. With each passing day, Michele knew she had to select a location for her new start and the clock was ticking

Michele sat up many a late night trying to figure out where the next chapter of her life should unfold. Her family wanted her to return home. The proposition of returning to Minnesota made her feel like she had failed with her life. If anything, the lessons learned while getting herself out of her marriage and the bad relationship proved Michele was not going to accept failure.

On the 29th day of her assignment selection period, Michele sat up late into the night. Looming over her head was an appointment with the Transportation Movement Office (TMO) at 0800 the next day. At this appointment, she had to give the assignment manager the desired destination of her household goods shipment or lose out on her relocation benefits. Inside, Michele was still unsure where the next chapter of her life's journey should be written. As she sat in her house on base in the midst of a maze of packed moving boxes, all the possibilities were crashing through her mind. It almost became too much. Pondering her next move, an idea came to her. Quickly Michele jumped to her feet and darted out the front door.

Michele ran across the front yard until she came to her parked car in the driveway. Inserting the key, she opened the passenger door. Rustling through the glove box she grabbed a tattered and torn copy of a Rand-McNally United States atlas. She returned to the nearly empty house and to her kitchen table. As she sat with the atlas closed in front of her she took a deep breath. She flipped the atlas haphazardly open. It landed on the map of Colorado. She paused, "Mmm the Rocky Mountain State." Then much like a child playing the game *Pin the Tail on the Donkey*, Michele closed her eyes. She took another deep breath, said a small prayer and randomly circled her finger over the map then rapidly pointed at a little town nestled in the Rockies, west of Denver. Slowly she focused her eyes on the map and read the name of her new hometown.

That town was called Leadville.

CHAPTER 10

Brian and Michele in Leadville

Michele enjoyed living in Leadville the past year and a half. The rustic little mountain hideaway had grown on her. She felt comfortable within the small-town setting. Some of the local residents and especially her family thought it strange that she felt accustomed to living in the little mountain community. After all, how could a girl who grew up surrounded by lakes feel at home cradled by the mountains? She did not waste much energy worrying about all of that. The bottom line to her was that Leadville felt comfortable and finally, she was at peace.

To make a living Michele worked at a specialty hiking and outdoors store. It was not a glamorous life, but everything she needed was there in Leadville. Her job provided just enough income to survive. What it did not produce in dollars and cents it made up for in enough free time to enjoy the surrounding mountains and trails. No longer worried about building a career or being the model wife, Michele focused her efforts on the present. Her failed marriage taught her to appreciate each day; as she learned firsthand, you never know what tomorrow could bring.

Life had settled down, became routine and predictable. Michele had grown happy and content in her new world. She enjoyed the easy-going pace of the remote mountain community. She lived alone in a nice two-bedroom cottage on East 11th Street just blocks from the center of town. Michele had accepted the single lifestyle and living alone. Other than a brief period when she lived on base, in the Airmen dorms, this was the first time she had established a home of her own. Michele felt proud about the life and residence she had established. Other than some companionship, Michele had everything she needed.

Besides the scars from her failed marriage, the only emotional baggage carried over from her time on Guam was the resonating loss over someone she had to leave behind. It always bothered her that in the disbanding of her marriage, the one that paid the highest price was her Daisy. Daisy was a beautiful young golden retriever who just loved to hang out and take walks on the beach. In the confusion of dissolving the marriage and unknown living arrangements, Daisy was given to friends. Michele reasoned that her faithful furry friend may have been the one who suffered the most. Michele always wondered about her and could not forget the look in Daisy's eyes when she said goodbye.

Since arriving in Leadville she'd had her guard up when it came to relationships with members of the opposite sex. Living in Leadville could get a little lonely. With a small-town population, if she wanted to start up a romance the dating options were limited. It did not take her long to realize that everyone knew everyone else. Being a young girl in town, she did not want her romantic interests to be town gossip. She was friendly but she kept to herself on matters of the heart. On one hand, she was happy with that; she did not need anything too exciting in her life. Still, there were times when Michele wondered if a companion, maybe a wet nosed companion like Daisy, would be fun.

One routine night, just as she had arrived home from work, the phone rang. The sound of the phone startled her as she struggled to get inside the door thinking the call may have been from her parents. As many times as she had told them her cell number they still always called her home phone. It had been a long day at work. Michele was tired and forgot about the caller ID. Within seconds of making her way through the doorway, the hard plastic phone receiver was resting against her check. As soon as she recognized the voice on the other end of the line, a cold chill made its way down her spine instantly she wished she had never answered the call. On the other end of the connection was her former husband. Michele could not believe the door to that life, one she thought she closed long ago, was suddenly reopened.

Over her protests, he told her he had been trying to contact her for quite some time. He mentioned he had almost given up until her brother provided her number. Michele never considered reconnecting with that part of her life and she sure would not have wanted him "trying" to get back into hers. Over her attempts to keep the conversation short, he told her that time had transformed him. He reasoned that being without her had allowed him to mature. He swore he was no longer "that" guy. All of his words sounded believable. She believed that everyone in life deserves a second chance. Maybe he had changed; after all. Michele knew she had changed. Until that phone call, she'd believed all of "that" life was behind her.

She said kindly but with resolve, "I'm really glad that you have gotten things together. It's just that" Michele paused to take a breath. "I'm not interested in revisiting that part of my life. We are best, I am best apart from you. Take care." The words barely left her lips as she hung up the phone. For her, it was time to move forward. With the cold click of the phone setting back down on its cradle, Michele hoped that the door to that stage of her life was finally closed and locked.

All of that conversation got lost as Michele switched her thoughts back to tonight's dinner plans. After the unplanned introduction on the trail, the two planned to have dinner, that very same evening. Michele's brain raced with thoughts and curiosity as she returned her focus to joining Brian for the "after collision" dinner. They planned to meet at one of the small diners, one that resembled an old Western storefront right off the screen of some 1960s Hollywood western. Michele nervously jitterbugged around her house getting ready and questioning everything she was going to wear. She paused long enough to wonder when the last time was that she cared about what she wore when she was going out. It had been a long time.

Not much had changed in Leadville since the booming days of the gold and silver rush. The majority of the downtown buildings appeared much like they did years ago. Brian and Michele sat opposite each other in a small wooden booth. The walls of the diner held relics from the town's mining days. Hung on the walls were black and white photos of those who had labored in the mines during the boom days. After their initial greetings and small talk around what they were ordering for dinner, there was an awkward pause in the conversation. To restart the exchange, Brian joked about their initial meeting. "Today on the trail, I saw my life flash before my eyes and I wondered who was going to let my dog out."

Michele smiled, "You have a dog?"

"Yes, I sure do. We are best friends. She keeps me company while I'm out on the road and it's nice knowing someone is missing me while I'm on the trails. Her name is Hanna." He stopped to clear his throat. "Hanna Lizbeth. She is a great little girl, a miniature schnauzer."

For two people who had just met, surprisingly once they started talking again the conversations were easy yet probing. They both had a strong desire to learn as much about the other as possible. Exchanging personal histories intermixed with tales from outdoor adventures, the time flew by almost unnoticed. The night may have started with Brian and Michele as near-perfect strangers but before long they were communicating like old friends with a kindred spirit.

Michele asked, "What brought you to Leadville Brian?"

"I'm here to run the 100. Why does anyone come to Leadville?" Brian paused, hoping that his reply was not to pointed. "How long have you lived here, Michele?" Brian quizzed back.

Michele laughed, "Well I've been here for a few years and I've never run the race." They both pause and studied each other's face.

Then Brian asked again, "What does bring you here? I can tell by your accent you're not from these parts."

"Well, I was trying to get away from something and Leadville just seemed like the place to be. Honestly, Leadville kind of picked me." Michele's voice turned quiet with her reply.

"That's good enough for me, Michele. That is a pretty name, only one L, I like that," Brian replied. Didn't the Beatles sing a song about you?"

Over dinner, they surprisingly found out they had a lot in common. They shared a sense of adventure. They both had a love of the outdoors. And sadly they both had experienced a loss in prior relationships.

As Brian sat across from her, he stole a glance of Michele's hazel eyes while she was not looking. When their eyes did connect, he felt drawn into her stare and noticed he enjoyed the sound of her northern Minnesota accent. Over the course of the night, enough details were uncovered that they realized they had each suffered hurt in past relationships. The night grew later and later. Michele noticed her watch and regretfully mentioned needing to be up early for work.

"Really? Then I'll be a good trail runner and won't keep you," Brian replied. "When are you running again? I want to be sure I'm on the lookout. "For a crazed squirrel, a wild bear or something crazy."

"That's funny really, I'm out there most days. Normally I hit the trails near the same time," Michele giggled. "Crazed squirrel, yea that's it…got to be careful."

They nervously got up from the table, slowly making their way to the door. Reaching the exit of the diner, they paused before walking out onto the sidewalk. Both were lost in how to classify this meeting and likewise confused and tentative on how it should end. Was this just a friendly dinner? Was the night a meeting of two people with similar interests? Brian had never been good at reading relationship signs or signals. He did not have much dating experience; Abby was Brian's one high school girlfriend. He never thought he would find himself in this situation again.

Michele made the first move. "I enjoyed tonight very much," she turned and said a second goodbye and walked out the door of the diner.

Brian was caught off-guard. A bit startled, he was standing flat-footed and at a loss for words. His mind was perplexed on how quickly the night ended. He trailed behind her, his mind blank on what to say. He had more questions he wanted to ask. He wanted to know everything about her. As fast as the initial collision had happened, Michele was now walking down the sidewalk. Before she was out of sight, she turned and waved. Brian smiled and waved back. Michele rounded the corner and turned east and was out of sight.

Brian stood in the middle of the sidewalk, with just six words racing through his mind: "I hope to see her again."

Continuing on her way home, Michele's mind got caught up in a blaze of questions. Most notably she began to question her standing on relationships. Was she ready to lower her guard? Was she hiding behind the failed relationship as a way of protecting herself? Did her life just get more complicated? She asked herself these questions and a number of others out loud in a series of rambling thoughts. "What just happened? Was that a date? Does he think that was a date?" What concerned her most was not Brian's answers to these questions, but her own. Was Michele considering this a date?

When Michele thought about the events leading up to the time she spent with Brian over dinner, her heart raced, she felt her face grow flushed and her pulse rate increased. "Two days ago, you were happy here alone. Now, what are you doing? Are you interested in this guy?" Her internal debate continued. He was nice. He seemed different. Walking the final yards to her front door, Michele looked towards the night sky. It was a clear night and the stars were shining brightly. She wondered if there might be something more to this simple dinner. "I haven't been out on a proper date since before I got married. Maybe it's time." Michele sensed something special with Brian and looked forward to spending more time with him in the future.

The next morning Brian woke up as the sun began to penetrate its way into the east facing windows. In the early morning stillness, his mind replayed all the events of the night before. As he rolled over, Hanna was startled from her slumber and looked back at him. "Hanna, what do you think?" He asked his faithful partner. For himself, he had a few more questions. "Am I ready for this? I've missed Abby so badly, but I want to share my life. I want to include someone and I want to be included." Hanna cuddled up next to his leg and before the day began they enjoyed a few moments just hanging out. Brian reached down and rubbed the soft fur on top of her head and between her ears. "Don't you worry girl, no matter what, you're my number one." Almost on cue, Hanna crawled on her belly and pushed her nose up under Brian's chin.

Reluctantly, the stillness of the morning broke. The first order of business was to get moving and get the puppy outside. After Hanna's morning routine was complete, it was time to enjoy breakfast. Brian grabbed a quick bite to eat, a couple rice cakes and some honey. While munching on his food he stole away some time to answer a few emails and edit a draft race report, the deadline of which was still a few days away. After about an hour of work and their bellies settled, it was time to head out on a run. For Hanna, it was time for her first nap of the day.

Brian quickly changed out of his street clothes and put on some running gear. As he finished lacing up his shoes, out of routine he told Hanna he would be back and to keep an eye on the fort. As he pulled the door shut he bent over and gave his little dog a comforting hug. Walking his way down the camp road which led to Route 4, Brian's mind was focused on the girl he had dinner with. Michele was foremost on his mind. With everything that was rolling over in his mind, it was truly time to go for a run. Brian knew he had a few things to work out, mainly his feelings. The open trails were the best place to sort out all of life's big questions.

The morning's plan was to run down Route 4 into Leadville along the same route the race would follow for its start and finishing legs. To simulate the race start, Brian wanted to run a segment from the starting location on 6th Street. From there he would follow the course to the May Queen Aid Station and then return to his campsite. A section of this run would cover the trails around Turquoise Lake, the same trails on which he had his fender-bender with Michele. Today he hoped they might cross paths again, either in town or out on the trail. Although getting ready for his training run, most of his attention was captured with thoughts of Michele. With a good amount of work in front of him, Brian knew he must get his focus on the task at hand.

Arriving at the trail head of Turquoise Trail, Brian paused to scan the area for any signs of Michele. Other than the sound of his own deep breathing, the trail head was eerily quiet. Not only were there no signs of Michele, there were no signs of anyone. For a weekday it was not uncommon for there to be a limited number of people out running or hiking, but today it looked as if the trail was Brian's alone.

Pausing for a moment in the stillness of the mountains, Brian daydreamed of what it may have been like if Michele was with him on the trail. He wondered what it would be like to spend the day running with her. Since they parted ways after dinner, she had been on his mind. He had considered calling her; he wanted to talk to her more and he hoped he would see her this morning. Realizing that daylight was burning, Brian snapped back to reality. "Enough of that, let's go. She is not here, Brian. We got nothing left but to get it done." On command, his feet pushed off from the packed trail surface. Reacting slowly at first, his legs propelled him down the trail until all his muscles came up to speed. The next thing Brian could think about was getting his legs up to high gear. "Alright Hanna dog, "this one is for you."

It was an outstanding workout. Brian's rapid leg turnover combined with the trail's undulating hills and Colorado's thin air all came together to open up his lungs. The focus of arriving in Leadville early was adapting to the high-altitude running that would be required during the race. Today, another thought occupied his mind as Brian neared the conclusion of this morning's run.

Arriving back at the trail head, Brian noticed the place was still desolate. There was no sign of anyone and on most days this would go unnoticed. Today Brian noticed. He looked around, scanned the parking lot and the bath houses. There was no one to be seen. Disappointed,

Brian mumbled under his breath, "Thought we might cross paths again, I was hoping she might be here." Nearly finished with his workout, Brian continued dejectedly back down the road that led to his campsite.

Brian returned back to his mobile studio apartment feeling good about his workout. Someone at the aluminum homestead was happy for his return. Walking up to the door, he could hear Ms. Hanna walking around in an excited fashion. Reaching to put the key into the lock, he noticed her nose pressed up on the glass window. "Good thing I don't mind cleaning that window over and over again, Hanna," he called out. He opened the door and two large brown eyes were staring at him. Hanna was always happy to see him. She was standing excitedly on her four legs with her cropped tail darting back and forth at a hundred miles an hour. Brian reached in and scooped her up into his arms. After a short hug, Hanna never seemed to mind if he was all sweaty, she licked his chin as Brian placed her on the ground. Once she was settled on her paws, they went for a short walk around the campground. Hanna loved being outside enjoying the sunshine and fresh air. Today was turning into a beautiful mountain day, and only one thing could make it better for Brian.

Not one to miss out on some fun and games with his best friend, Brian sat down on a chair next to the campfire ring. Finding a small stick he tossed it out in front of Hanna. Instantly her ears perked up and in rapid motion, she pounced on the stick for a very heated game of keep-away. As much as she loved to fetch and return, she equally liked to pretend to return the stick just to run away with it again. The two had a few precious minutes of playful fun and then it was time to get cleaned up. "Okay, girl, you win," he called out to her. "I need to get cleaned up, so back inside we go." Brian planned to go into town. He needed a few food items and may just need a few things at the hiking & outdoor store. Reasoning he may need some back-up, Brian thought it would be a good idea to bring Hanna along on the shopping trip.

Walking through the door of a weathered storefront, an old-fashioned bell sounded overhead. The sound transported Brian back in time to the

1970s. The store carried all the latest outdoor gear and high-tech hiking equipment, but the atmosphere felt rustic and dated compared to the modern big-box retail climate of today. Taking two steps inside, the creaking wooden floors welcomed him. As his eyes adjusted to the lighting, he scanned the interior. Hanna pranced in behind him and for a moment, Brian wondered if this was dog-friendly environment.

Brian liked the old-world charm, a general store feeling out of the old mountain west. In one corner of the store, a stuffed grizzly bear was standing upright in a very aggressive posture. Hanna and Brian noticed the bear almost at the same time and both took a step back. "Can I help you?" an unseen female voice rang out from behind the counter, breaking their surprise.

Brian was pretty sure he recognized that voice. His heart rate increased as he smiled with his reply, "Sure, I need a bear whistle to let people, I mean, bears know I'm on the trail. Someone, I mean a bear ran me over the other day."

"Oh, it's you." Michele came from around the counter.

Brian replied with a smile. "Yeah just me…well and Hanna dog."

Michele's eyes lit up when she saw Brian's traveling companion walking innocently behind him. "Oh, I see you brought Ms. Hanna." Michele knelt down to greet the furry little friend. "Are you trying to win some brownie points?"

"I'll take any points I can get. Is it okay that she is in here?"

After some shy chit-chat, Michele and Brian talked about the outdoors, his ultra running and her adventures hiking and running the trails of her new hometown. The small talk continued when Brian asked her how she enjoyed their dinner. "Oh I had a blast," Michele admitted, then off-guard she continued, "I've been thinking about you ever since. I mean about the dinner." And with a coy smile, Michele turned in the other direction.

"Oh, me too, I mean about the dinner," chuckled Brian. He walked around the store trying to find the few items he intended on purchasing. Hanna followed him, steering clear of the menacing bear. Then he turned back towards Michele and asked a serious question. "So Michele with one L, you never told me why you came to Leadville?"

"Well, it's a long story, but I'll get right to the punch line," Michele boldly replied. "I was getting out of the military and not sure where I wanted to live. One night my finger pointed to this place on the map. Leadville seemed as good a place as any. Most importantly, it's where my abusive ex-husband is not." Her words hung in the air, seconds felt like hours. Brian's eyes caught hers after Michele offered up such a deep and personal look into her life.

"Oh, I'm sorry. I did not mean to pry. I shouldn't have asked such a pointed question…" Brian now diverted his sight to the creaking hardwood floor as he nervously hoped he did not ask the wrong question.

"No, it's okay…you didn't do anything wrong. Leadville was the perfect place to get away and start over. I like it here." Michele quickly filled in the dead space.

"So do I, Michele. Are you running again anytime soon? I'll tell you my life story, but it has to be on the trails. I just can't do it here," Brian responded back.

"Sure, how's tomorrow?" I have the morning off and could use a few miles, after that food you made me eat the other night" Michele offered up.

"Deal, I'm there." As Brian paid for his items, he smiled looking intently into her eyes and then thanked her for being open and honest. Motioning for Hanna, Brian turned to walk towards the door.

Michele asked, "Hey there, Ms. Hanna you're not going to go without saying goodbye?" Michele walked around the counter separating the two and followed them as they made their way to the door. Brian stopped while Hanna turned to Michele, who gave Hanna one big ear-ruffling rub on the top of her head.

As Brian made a turn for the door, Michele reached out as if to shake his hand. Instinctively to meet her move, his hand reached out to hers. They both touched in an awkward half shake, half holding onto each other's hand. Her skin felt soft, tender and electric to his touch. He wanted to hold onto her and not let go. He also did not want to misread any signals. Brian smiled as he turned to walk out the door "Can't wait for tomorrow, Michele."

"I'll be there," Michele replied.

Back at the campsite, Brian took advantage of the early start of his day to settle in for a midday nap. That was one of the many advantages to the low-cost lifestyle he led. As long as his editors were happy, deadlines were met, and Hanna had a full belly, his time was his to enjoy. A couple hours passed and it was time to straighten up around his site, get some firewood and put together a few things for dinner. Once all the busy work was done it was time to start a fire and enjoy the late afternoon hours.

Brian sat back and relaxed in his camp chair. It was not long before Hanna noticed and wanted to join him. Jumping up, Hanna then walked a few circles in Brian's lap until she found a comfortable place. Settling down, she soon went off to sleep. Meanwhile, Brian stared off into the western sky and the clear view of the mountains. Every once in a while Hanna lifted her head, looked back at him while he talked to her about his life. "Hanna-girl, am I ready for this?" A few moments passed and Hanna laid her head back down on his lap. "I haven't been this interested in anyone since…" He paused; Hanna lifted her head again and looked at him. "You know, since Abby." The conversation broke off. Hanna stared back into his eyes, paused, tilted her head just a bit then lowered her head back onto his leg. "Yeah, I understand, Hanna. I'm tired too." Brian and Hanna passed much of the remainder of the night staring into the fire.

In the morning, it was time to meet Michele at the trail head. Brian was nearly out of his mind with eager anticipation to get this run started, not so much for the workout or the miles he would later enter in his training logbook. Today he was more excited about the prospect of spending additional time with Michele. As he waited for her to arrive, his heart rate climbed to near cardiac proportions. He was nearly out of breath. Brian was very excited to see where this new relationship may go, but also a bit tentative about going too fast or expecting too much.

As Michele climbed out of her car, Brian glanced at his watch. She was right on time. He liked that trait and noticed her bright smile. Her presence alone brightened up the almost perfect morning. The morning sky was filled with blue skies and warm sunshine. Today nothing in nature would capture his attention as much as Michele would.

Brian wondered if there was ever a bad morning in the high altitudes of the Colorado Rockies. The trail was in good shape, packed and with just enough moisture for a soft footfall that kept the dust from being kicked up. There was not much that could make this outing any more picture perfect.

Michele walked over from her parking spot, smiled and began the conversation. "Morning! I've been looking forward to this run ever since we set it up. I could hardly sleep last night."

As Michele walked his way, the first thing he noticed after her beaming smile, was that she showed up in some cool running gear. Michele wore a pair of black high-tech shorts and a gray technical shirt featuring the logo of the Bolder Boulder 10k. Her shoe of choice for the day was a pair of red and white aggressive trail shoes topped off with a pair of gaiters featuring neon colored bows. In her hand was a hand carried waterbottle.

Brian stammered his response. "Ah, yeah…yeah me too." He finally got his words to come out clear. "I take it you have run the 10k, I've got that race on my list." With a little extra motivation, they both took off together down the trail.

"It is an awesome race, I highly recommend it," Michele replied as they began their run.

This morning, the cadence of their foot strike meshed together perfectly. Without much effort, Michele stayed side by side with Brian. Today was not about setting new training times, running fartlek's or tempo runs, today was an easy run day. They made their way out on the trail at a pace that allowed their conversations to flow smoothly. The physical effort was balanced between not interfering with the spoken words or the thought patterns needed to string the appropriate thoughts together.

"Today we shouldn't have much of a problem knocking each other to the ground since we're side by side, right." Brian tossed off a zinger.

Brian was relieved he found a running partner that appeared accomplished on the trails. Although this was not a business run, within the first few strides his trained eye picked up on Michele's graceful and efficient gait.

Somewhere along the run, the conversation turned from the lighthearted and easy-to-talk about subjects to the most penetrating chapters of life. As the discussion probed deeper, the next thing Brian knew, he was recounting about how he first fell in love. He was telling Michele about a girl named Abby. Brian related how Abby made him feel complete for the first time in his life.

As the pair made their way along the trail, Brian felt at ease and told Michele nearly his complete life story. He told her about his parent's divorce and the painful rejection at the hands of his father. He tried to explain that for most of his life he'd wondered if anyone could love him. His voice broke when he told her about his deep feelings for Abby and that she was the one that he had planned to marry. He was certain; she was the one for him at that time in his life. Brian concluded that unfortunately, sadly for him, that time had passed.

Michele tenderly asked, "When did she break up with you?"

"She." He paused to catch his breath and to regain his composure. The two still moving at a leisurely pace along the trail. "She didn't break up with me." As Brian paused to catch his breath, Michele noted his breathing became erratic. Brian replied rather quietly. "She died." He completed what may have been the most difficult sentence of his life. The impact of those words, that statement took her breath away. She was caught completely off-guard. Michele stopped mid-stride. Brian followed her lead and turned back to face her, emotions building up in his eyes.

"Oh, Brian, I'm so sorry. Please forgive me."

"Of course, it's okay, you had no idea. You had no way of knowing." They both stood facing each other, motionless and speechless.

Breathing deeply, Brian encouraged Michele to start running again. As they headed back out on the trail, he began to explain. "It was a normal Sunday morning. We were running along a road we had run together a number of times. Then there was this sound."

By the time Brian had shared all the intimate details of his time with Abby, they were back at the trailhead. The morning run had covered 15 miles. The emotional toll on both of them made it feel like they had ran 25 or 50. They both came to a stop. No one was speaking; they just stood there uncomfortably looking at the ground. The time felt like hours when in fact it was only seconds. The emotional conversation taxed both of them, but they were happy they had a chance to talk. Brian was happy Michele got to know a deeper side to him and his life. Michele then made the first move.

Michele's voice broke the silence. "I enjoyed our run today, Brian, thank you for opening up to me." She paused to catch her breath, "I'm so sorry for your loss, but in a way I understand. When my husband started hitting me it was very much like the death of someone I loved." With those words, she reached forward and hugged Brian. "If you need me, give me a call.

"Okay. Thank you, I think I'll just walk back to camp. I need a few moments."

"I understand. See you again?"

CHAPTER 11

A New Relationship

The next day while Brian was navigating the streets of the old, rustic mining town he saw Michele out running errands. He stopped her and asked if she wanted to have dinner or to just hang out. "Hanna wants to see you, again," he stated. They both laughed and she agreed.

"It won't be anything fancy, some turkey burgers on the grill and sweet potato fries. If we are lucky, Hanna might share some kibble with us if that's not enough." Brian chuckled.

Michele agreed and said she would be over around 7 p.m. "Perfect. It's a date." He replied. "I'll have the fire going. Would you bring some marshmallows?"

With those words, "a date," there was a pause in the conversation. They looked at each other and smiled. As Brian and Michele parted ways, returning to their daily routine, he reached out and touched the back of Michele's right hand. "I can't wait to see you again."

Time flew by surprisingly fast. Brian found that he was happy on one hand and a bit conflicted on the other. He did not want to think about this "date" too much. He enjoyed being with Michele and at the same time, felt a bit uneasy when he considered starting up another relationship. His feelings for Abby had been hard for him to deal with. They were still very raw. He missed her. He also knew he wanted to and needed to move on. It saddened him that he never really had the opportunity to express how deeply he loved her. What hurt him the most was he never got to say goodbye. There was no closure.

Michele arrived at the campsite and parked her car behind Brian's truck, along the front of the camper. Out of her car, she walked around towards the back of the site and noticed the blazing fire that was waiting for her. She also noticed Hanna sitting in a camp chair. Hanna perked right up the moment Michele came into view. She did not bark, but got very excited and made enough noise rustling about that Brian knew he had a visitor. He stuck his head out of the back door and instantly saw Michele bending over patting Hanna on the head and ruffling the fur down her back.

Seeing the two interacting, Brian called out. "You better watch it, she ate the last person who came up here," he joked.

"I'll take my chances. It's good to see you," Michele replied.

This time Brian did not let his cold feet or cautious demeanors keep him from acting. He smartly came right out of the camper, approached Michele and confidently gave her a big hug. "It's great, really great to see you."

Michele enjoyed the hug and matched his brave move with a light kiss on the check. Feeling left out on the greetings, Hanna barked. "Yeah, little one, you'll get some attention too, I promise," Brian responded back to his faithful companion.

The night went along perfectly. Although very nervous, Brian thought the evening could not have played out better. The couple enjoyed a great meal and conversations. They continued to learn about each other's upbringing, past, and dreams for the future. They also found that they had a lot in common. Michele found out Brian was a great camp site-cook. He couldn't boil water on a conventional stove but give him a campfire or gas grill and he was at home. The conversations progressed, bouncing from personal histories to current attentions and attractions. They talked as if they were very comfortable with each other and never at a loss for words. Brian and Michele had so much to learn about one another that time passed rapidly.

After dinner, they sat back in reclining camp chairs and talked more about life. Michele asked Brian about how he met Abby, about her family, his childhood and how he felt without her. Michele shared her thoughts about her failed marriage and her military career. She also offered insight on what she thought went right and wrong with being married. She also exposed why she felt comfortable in Leadville. Brian and Michele discovered that although they arrived in Leadville on very different paths, those paths converged at perhaps the perfect place and time.

They spent the rest of the night staring at the evening sky with Hanna sandwiched between them.

"So you really live in your camper full-time?" Michele asked him out of the blue.

"Yes, I haven't found anywhere that feels like home. So I take my home with me. With Hanna and I, it's perfect. My job allows me to travel and I'm able to work anywhere that has WiFi. There's a lot of freedom and it's much cheaper than a stick-and-brick home. It works for me…and for right now," Brian explained.

"I guess I understand," Michele replied. "You get paid to write about running."

"Yeah, crazy, I know…but again it works for me. I run. I write and they pay me. It's a tough life."

"So what is on your agenda for tomorrow, Mr. Camper Man?" They both kind of laughed that off.

"Well, funny you should ask. Nothing. It's a rest day for me. I plan to sleep in late. By late, I mean like maybe 7 a.m. and then do nothing but play with my little girl right here." Hearing those words, Hanna picked her head up almost on cue. "You see, I have a 50-mile run planned in two days and need to get some rest in."

"Ah, love me some rest days," Michele replied, "You looking for company?"

"Tomorrow? You'll have to ask Hanna," he joked.

"No, silly, for the long run. I can't run it all but would be up for meeting you along the way," Michele suggested with a beaming smile.

"Sure…plus, Hanna would not be up for sharing me tomorrow. We have a serious game of go fetch to play."

"I wouldn't think about getting in the way of that." Michele smiled at Hanna. "A girl needs her time with her special guy."

For the remainder of the evening, the two sat side-by-side staring at the campfire. As the glowing orange and amber hue of burning logs crumbled into ash, the stars slowly began to appear in the dark mountain sky. It was comforting for Brian to be in Michele's presence. Covertly he stole a glance at her when she wasn't looking. Hanna grew tired of playing with her ball and sniffing around the campsite. She found her way onto Michele's lap. Brian reached over and tapped the back of her hand. "I think she likes you." Brian nodded in Hanna's way.

"I like her too."

Brian did not remove his hand from Michele's after her response.

Returning their attention to the campfire and the approaching night sky, Brian and Michele sat in the stillness and warmth of the fire. "I don't want this night to end," Brian thought to himself.

Michele forced herself to break away from the moment she noted how late it had become. She remembered that she did not have a rest day, but needed to open the store. "Brian I've had a great night, thank you so much. Thank you, Ms. Hanna, for sharing your special guy. So where should I meet you?"

Brian explained, "You know where the Aid Station is near Twin Lakes? I plan to run out and back from the MayQueen Aid Station. If you wouldn't mind could you drive out there and we could run back together? We could then clean up and get some food, then go back out and get your car?"

"Sure, that sounds like a plan," Michele replied. The two set up a time and finalized the details. Standing up, Michele patted Hanna on her head. She then stepped towards Brian and gave him a long hug. As their embrace broke, Michele placed a kiss on his lips.

"This was great, thank you. Best night I've had in a long time." Brian beamed with his reply.

As Michele walked back to her car Brian picked up Hanna and held her firmly against his chest so they both could see. Michele settled into the driver's seat and looked out the side window. Her warm smile and the taste of her kiss still fresh on his lips told him everything he needed to know. He had stolen her heart. As Michele pulled away, Brian waved with Hanna's paw held firmly in his hand. He also remembered how soft Michele's lips felt on his.

"Wow, Hanna, isn't she great?" Hanna looked up at Brian and rolled her head under his chin in that puppy love kind of way. "I think she liked you too and that is just as important. Hanna, do you think Abby would like her?"

With that, Brian put Hanna into the camper as he tended to the fire before calling it a night. Right before going inside, he looked up at the stars. "Abby do you?" Brian paused to stop his voice from breaking. "Do you like her? Is this okay?"

The following day, the two were just about back from Twin lakes. Nearing the end of their long run, Brian looked over at Michele, commenting, "It's been a great run. You're looking strong at nearly 25 miles."

Michele was a newcomer to ultra-distance running, although she had run several marathons. Brian noticed that she was at home on the trails and the high elevations of Leadville. "Yeah, I didn't want to make you look too bad out there." Those words barely got out of her mouth and off her lips when she took off at a good clip. Brian was left wondering what was going on. He was caught off-guard, but not for long. Just as fast as Michele exposed her get-away move, his brain figured out he had a race on his hands. Falling behind ignited Brian's very competitive side. He was determined to catch her.

"Oh, that's not nice, missy." Brian pressed his right foot into the ground and planted hard with a firm push off. The jagged trend pattern of his trail shoes instantly bit into the dirt surface, got traction and propelled his body forward throwing off a small chunk of dirt behind him in the process. Within a single stride, his legs hit high gear. An easy and rapid leg turnover began to draw her in. Within an eighth-of-a-mile he pulled up next to her, "Oh yeah, Michele, you're like that, are you" then he playfully patted her on the butt as he passed by.

Almost instantly he wondered if he took his playfulness too far? Did he upset her, with such personal contact? All of those questions were left on the trail when Michele returned the favor as she zinged past him. Then she jumped a short-cut, bounded over a log and was off the trail first. This little surprise race ended with Michele being the victor.

If it wasn't for the fact that Brian hated to lose at anything, he would have fallen to the ground laughing. Michele was so happy because of her little victory, she danced around in a circle prancing up and down singing out like a school-girl. "I won, I won and I beat you!" Her little celebration broke through his competitive side. Brian just smiled at her with sweat running down from his forehead. He was really not too sure about this girl, but he did know that he liked her, a lot.

Walking over to congratulate her, Brian replied. "You got me. You sure did." Michele, lost in the excitement, bounced right up to him wrapping her arms around his neck in a big old bear hug. Reactions took over when Brian felt Michele hugging him. He instinctively placed his arms around the small of her small waist and pulled her in tight. For a second, time stood still as they were both lost in the embrace.

Brian noticed how firm and light she was. To him, it felt good to hold her in his arms. He didn't want to let her go. He also did not want the moment to be clumsy or awkward. Brian regretfully began to release his arms from around her. Then as they began to break contact, Michele pulled him in giving him a big and rather sweaty kiss. Michele got one last parting shot in: "I beat you" rang out in his ear. She laughed a bit as she pulled away.

Inside Brian instantly broke into a debate with himself. "What just happened? Well, she beat you in a race dummy. No kidding, but what about that hug? What about the kiss? Man, she is pretty, was that a likes me hug and kiss or? Man, you let a girl beat you. I don't care, what about that hug?"

Finally, his brain re-engaged with the real world and he thanked Michele for the run and asked what her plans were for dinner. "I figure since I'm the loser here, he said," with a devilish grin on his face, "I need to take you out for dinner?"

"Well, I am kind of hungry," Michele replied. "You know us, runners, we can always eat. I think they call it being rungry!"

"Okay, then let's say 7 p.m., your choice," He offered, realizing he was getting the better end of the deal.

"Deal, I know this great little steak and barbecue place just outside of town." Michele got in one last shot. "Did you know I beat you?"

The excitement of the impromptu race had passed, after cleaning up and a quick recovery snack, Brian was pulling into the parking lot and walking Michele to her car. Standing facing each other, he was conflicted on the amount of physical affection he should show her. He debated a simple goodbye hug or not. Should he lean in and kiss her? He did not want to overstep any boundaries, but he also wanted to show her how much he cared.

He had always felt shy and uncomfortable knowing what the next move should be when faced with a romantic situation. As the stillness between them began to break, Michele reached out for another hug and to say goodbye. Something overtook Brian's normally conservative nature. He made his move. As she moved forward, his hand reached out and softly cradled her face. He paused for one second, looking deep into her eyes, then slowly gave Michele a full, well-placed kiss on her lips. After this more personal exchange, she stepped back and smiled. "Well, I guess you like me...like me." They both laughed. Brian was a bit embarrassed.

As they departed Michele, looked back at Brian and softly said, "That was nice."

For the next two weeks, they spent nearly all their free time together, running the trails, walking around Leadville and spending time with Hanna. Within the outdoors and running community, it was noticed that they both took a fondness for each other. Many of Michele's friends noticed that they were always together. A few remarked what a wonderful couple they were. What started out as a casual long run had turned into a deep and personal connection. Brian knew he liked Michele a lot. He also knew that he needed to move slowly. For himself, his still tender feelings for Abby could not be just put aside. Brian wanted to show her the respect she deserved and that he held for her. He knew it was time to move on from the hurt and loss of his past. He knew if fate had turned the cards 180 degrees he would have wanted Abby to find love again. Brian knew he wanted to love again and to share his life with someone.

Michele also desired to proceed slowly over any romantic course they might be on. She knew Brian was different than her ex. She felt a deeper connection than she had with anyone before. But she wasn't a girl who would allow a physical relationship to outpace the deeper emotional one. Not to say they were not tender and affectionate; they both loved to hold hands and never let each other part without a hug and an affectionate kiss. On hold was the deeper, more intimate part of a male-female interpersonal relationship and they both accepted that.

The quality of the time they got to spend together got better and better as the days, nights and weekends rolled along. Then one night while sitting around the campfire, Brian had some news to share. "Michele, so if I told you I robbed a bank and was heading to jail, would you wait around for me?"

Michele looked at him with an expression on her face as if he had just lost his mind. "Ah, not for long. What have you done Butch Cassidy, robbed the local stagecoach or held up the federal bank?"

Brian replied at first in laughter, "No nothing like that." Then his voice grew serious. "Well, my editor called today. He asked if I could cover a trail running camp for the next two weeks. I have to be there in three days. If I leave tomorrow, I can get there in time."

Michele's eyes grew sad. She was shocked and a slightly heartbroken. She was also supportive in her reply. "Well, not the best news, I understand. You did tell me that was part of your life." She nervously bite her lip and looked towards the ground. "It is kind of fast. Do these assignments always come on so quickly? I mean this is only a few days notice."

"Yes. That is the drawback of being mobile. I can turn the job down, but I do get a lot of my assignments that way. On the flipside, it does pay pretty good money. I WILL be coming back. It's a perfect fit between now and the 100. Plus I get to run all the training runs with the camp coaches for free. And hey, we both like free."

"Brian, I understand. I can't say I'm happy. I'm going to really miss you. Go do what you need to, but be sure to come back. If something comes up." Michele paused. "If you don't come back please just give me a call, I've grown kind of fond of seeing you. I really enjoy our time together." A heaviness hung over the conversation as Michele's eye grew moist.

Brian stood up and approached Michele who was still seated in her chair. He bent down beside her on one knee. Looking into her eyes, and holding her hand Brian told her, "Michele, I have every intention to come back." Feeling the now present tension in the air, he attempted to break the ice. "Hanna made me promise to come back. I can't let the little dog down. Nor could I ever dream of a world, my world where I would not see you again."

The rest of the night they sat side by side, Hanna sandwiched in between. As they stared at the fire, the two held hands long into the night. The warmth of the fire combined with the crackling sounds from the red-hot embers was hypnotic. All three fell asleep under the mountain sky.

It's a bit of a surprise to find one's self outside sitting in a reclining camp chair. That is exactly what happened when a barking Hanna woke them up. "Hey girl, what's going on?" A random squirrel had made its way into camp and was eyeing up the bag of leftover peanuts from the night before. It was a good thing Hanna alerted everyone. Michele had just enough time to get home, clean up and get to work. Brian and Hanna had to get busy too. Brian needed to break down camp and get on the road.

Upon saying goodbye, Michele and Brian held the deepest embrace they had since starting down this road as a couple. Brian promised her they would see each other again. Even with the reassurance, Michele left with tears in her eyes and her heartbreaking. Brian, although distracted with tearing down camp, felt much the same. Inside he knew he would be back, but he hated the idea of leaving for any length of time just the same.

Brian was proud of the efficiency in which he could break camp, pack up his gear and get on the road. Since choosing this compact and mobile lifestyle he had had a lot of practice. He had become a master logistician at packing out and deploying his mobile home to its next location. Today it all went too fast. In relatively no time the camper was secured and tied down with all his items stowed away. Before leaving the campgrounds, Brian settled up his bill and made arrangements for his return. The owner promised to hold his site. They had grown fond of him as he was always polite and helpful around camp. In less than two hours the bright silver dually was on the road. As he drove out of town, Hanna walked a few circles on the seat next to him searching for the perfect spot. Once a spot was to her liking she lazily plopped down. His traveling companion had found a comfortable place to enjoy the ride. Brian's heart was breaking.

As the truck and camper combination made its way onto the interstate that would lead them to the next adventure, Brian's emotions were on edge. He kept telling himself that this was just two short weeks. The words did nothing to ease his pain, he hurt so badly. There were many questions intermixed in his thoughts. Would everything be the same when he got back? Did they care for each other enough? Was this really a relationship? Did he have what it took to move on from the first love of his life? All he knew for sure was that he had intense feelings for Michele and that there was a self-imposed and very painful hole in his chest. Although he knew he would be returning to Leadville and Michele, Brian felt empty inside as the modest former mining town grew small in the rearview mirror.

CHAPTER 12

Returning to Leadville

During the time away from Leadville, Brian came to terms with his growing love for Michele. He also reconciled the internal conflict he felt about closing the final chapter of his life with Abby. He was determined to give his relationship with Michele everything he had. He felt blessed to find love again. At one point in the dark days after Abby's passing, he questioned if he could love anyone again. Returning to Leadville, Brian felt he had been given a second chance. He believed Michele was special because with her love and with her understanding of Abby's place in his life, he would be able to move forward.

Abby would always be a part of Brian's life. Michele knew that and she did not see Abby as a rival. After all, Abby nurtured an insecure boy into a confident, caring and loving man. Brian had been praying for a future filled with love, compassion, acceptance, and understanding. During the time he got to spend with Michele, he came to terms that his future would be found with this wonderful blonde-haired, hazel-eyed girl with just a hint of a Northern accent. With each passing day, he grew more confident that he wanted to pursue a serious relationship with this girl from Minnesota. Smitten by this beautiful girl with a tender soul, he looked forward to his return to Leadville. Departing the Lake Tahoe area, Brian believed for the first time in a long time that he was traveling in the right direction. Not only was Brian traveling back to Leadville, he was also on his way back to Michele.

With his assignment and the follow-up article submitted, Brian was headed back to the old-time mining town, stopping only to refuel with diesel, caffeine and an occasional junk food treat. These high energy staples would ensure he'd be back in town as soon as possible. With the extended fuel tanks and a six-pack of empty Mountain Dew cans littered on the floorboards, Brian arrived in Colorado three days before the race.

While apart, Brian and Michele had kept in near constant contact. They talked for hours on end, exhausting their cell phone plans. They also leveraged internet chatting, messaging and real-time video connections. Even though they were apart, Brian believed he grew closer to Michele. Through those conversations, while sharing intimate details, they both yielded a deeper union. Brian found it easy to share information with her and his fondness for Michele grew with every interaction whether in person or on the other end of modern technology which helped bridge the gap.

His modern day wagon train would be returning to the same campground that served as base camp just weeks before. Passing the white-washed concrete sign with the words "We ♥ Leadville ~ Great Living at 10,200 feet," a comfortable, secure feeling returned to his spirit. Brian knew one thing for certain; he couldn't wait to see Michele. Besides navigating his way along Interstate highways I-80 and I-70 Brian had been burning up the cell phone towers devising a master plan to surprise her. He arrived back in town a day earlier than expected.

Pulling into camp, Brian stopped to talk with the hosts, who had been expecting him. They were a young couple, Dennis and Sue, who were happy to see him return as they had hit it off during his last stay. They managed the site. Like Brian they lived and worked full-time out of their RV. They understood his mobile nature. After some small talk, they directed him to the same spot he occupied just a few weeks before.

Hearing some familiar voices, Hanna jumped to her feet and peered out the window. "Hey, girl, are we home?" As those words were spoken out loud, Brian paused and reflected for a moment. The statement rang in his ears. *Home.* For a long time, that word had an empty feeling to it. Today when Brian heard those words vocalized, there was finally a peaceful and comfortable feeling behind them.

While navigating to his spot that Brian noticed the increase in activity as the race date drew near. Backing the truck onto the concrete pad, Brian glanced over his shoulder to ensure that his camper was square on the site. Satisfied he had it as level as possible, he shut down the engine to begin the manual set-up. With Hanna in tow, he went about the work of turning his rolling home on wheels into a comfortable studio apartment. With a simple hand-held controller, not much more than a TV remote, he directed the operation. With the push of a simple button, four electric motors sprung to life, rotating jackscrews that ran the four camper stabilizer legs down. Brian then unhooked four tie-down chains and fine-tuned the camper jackscrews to achieve a level condition. Next came the high pitch of a hydraulic pump feeding pressurized fluid through lines that expanded the actuating cylinders that positioned the slide-outs. These slide-outs along the right side of the camper expanded the living area to near double the size. All these actions transformed the simple aluminum box in the bed of Brian's truck into a rolling condominium.

Brian's mobile stateroom had a dinette on the right side and an expanded kitchen on the left. A full shower and bath occupied the rear. It may have felt cramped to some, but for Brian and Hanna, their home was perfect. During the commotion of set-up, Hanna oversaw the whole operation. As the four-legged foremen, if she did not like the way things were progressing she would lie down and take a nap until it was over. They made a wonderful team. "Home. Sweet. Home. What do you think, Hanna?" Brian called out to his co-pilot. After unpacking his gear and, connecting the water, electric, and sewer lines, his campsite was quickly established. Pausing for just a second, Brian looked over to the mountains and marveled at how everything just felt familiar. Everything was comfortable. Everything felt like home.

After finishing up all the checklist items to finalize his living arrangement, he clipped Hanna onto her lead and called out, "Let's go for a walk." Hanna instantly went from her calm and easy going self to an excited little camper dog. His little girl jumped right up, excitedly pranced around in a little circle and with a full body doggie shake, they were off walking around camp. Brian and Hanna made the rounds visiting the staff and the other campers they met during their last stay.

Everyone liked Hanna. As she made her rounds many of the other guests responded to her by name. With Hanna near, it was pretty clear Brian was the supporting cast member and he was happy in this role. Brian enjoyed seeing his dog get all the attention and reconnect with some good people. Meanwhile, his mind was distracted with the big surprise he had waiting.

After the homecoming lap with Hanna, it was time for Brian to clean up and get ready to head into town. He had been anticipating this day nearly since the wheels of his truck first rolled out of Leadville.

As race day drew near, the pace of life in town bristled with activity. As he walked the familiar streets, Brian noticed the increase in energy and the positive vibe in the air. With the influx of ultra runners, this normally calm little hamlet nestled in the mountains had come alive. Making his way further into town, he occasionally stopped to tap on a few store-front windows to say hello to the shopkeepers. In his short time there he made a lot of friends; it felt as if he had been a part of the community for years. Life in Leadville had been settling, it had been calming and it had been good for Brian.

While walking past a glass pane window of a small grocery store, Brian paused as something caught his attention. For a second he just stared at the reflected figure. The likeness peering back at him he knew well, although, in some ways, this likeness appeared completely new. The familiar face gazing back looked revitalized. The reflection was highlighted by a spark in his eyes that months ago was missing. An extra lift in his smile was the centerpiece of an appearance that looked alive, energized and not simply living. Brian had only felt this way once, before. Breaking the stare, he confirmed to himself out loud, "Abby would have wanted you to live. She would not have wanted you to be alone. Michele is a great girl." As he made his way deeper into town he felt his walking pace pick up. Brian anticipated that this was a turning point in his life.

After the tragic loss, Brian reluctantly grew comfortable being alone. He got used to his own company. At some point, he even rationalized that he may spend the rest of his life alone. Michele changed all of that. Michele changed his perspective and how he viewed his life looking forward.

During the time Brian was on assignment at the running camp, away from Michele, the solitude allowed his mind to process everything that happened between them. Realizing he did not have to settle for being on his own, his heart truly opened up to the idea of a new relationship. Inside he knew he had fallen for Michele. Free from any guilt or reservations, it was easy to embrace the feeling of loving someone again. Brian admitted to himself the need for the intimacy and security of sharing his life.

He admitted to himself that he was indeed in love.

As Brian walked towards a local diner, he was finally ready to move forward with life. He felt confident life should encompass a future with the girl who nearly ran him over on the trail. He finally understood and accepted that it was Michele who made him feel whole again.

It was approaching dinner time. Moving briskly, Brian couldn't wait to see the girl who had won over his spirit and stole his heart. He could not wait, to see Michele. He wanted to tell her everything that he had thought about while away. He wanted to tell her he was ready. He desperately wanted to tell her he wanted to build a new life with her.

Brian approached the family-owned diner just off of Second Street.

Days earlier on the way back to Leadville, he called The Outdoor Store where Michele worked and with the help of a friend and co-worker arranged a surprise meeting over dinner. Walking up to the front door of the diner, Brian was confident the surprise was going to go off without compromise.

It was a cute and cozy Victorian house where the two of them had eaten at once before. Brian remembered the food was good, with a Mexican flair. He had the sizzling chicken fajitas, she had the California burrito. He also recalled it was fun sitting behind one of the framed windows watching the neighbors coming and going. It was majestic viewing the mountain skylines while they ate.

Reaching for the door, he pulled it open and took a step inside. It took a few seconds for his eyes to adjust to the lighting. Then he scanned the room looking for the profile of her beautiful familiar face. The dining area was about half full. In the background were the traditional sounds of plates and eating utensils coming together. Doubt entered his mind. Was his information flawed? Did Michele decide to eat at home tonight, he wondered. Then a figure across the room caught his attention. The room went quiet. All perceivable sound disappeared. The only thing Brian was able to hear was the sound of his chest expanding as he breathed and the pulsating action of his heart.

Out of the corner of his eye Brian's focus was drawn toward two people sitting together. He could clearly hear his heart skip a beat. Then a jolt of adrenaline rocketed through his veins. For a split second, he was elated to see Michele; he had no doubt it was her. He recognized her smile and the outline of her face. Those eyes. The eyes that stole his heart caught his attention. He knew it was her. Then something appeared wrong. Questions rang out in his mind.

Who was that other figure? His breathing increased and the only sound that was audible was the precision beating of his heart. What is going on? The question echoed violently in his mind. Everything in his world stopped, frozen in time. He blinked his eyes to ensure he saw what he had thought he saw. Then the world began to turn again, it began spinning and not in a good way. Brian's mind couldn't process what his eyes were seeing. It went against everything he had hoped for.

The two figures were sitting at a small table positioned in the far corner of the room. His mind reeled and his world was thrown off balance. Who was she sitting with? They looked a little too familiar to him. They sat a little too close and they looked a little too comfortable to be strangers. The stranger's hand reached for hers. Time paused again and this time it felt like hours but was only seconds. The stranger's head turned ever so slightly, then all the connections were instantly made. Sitting with Michele was her former husband. Brian recognized him from the wedding photos she shared one evening while explaining what went wrong in her marriage.

Not understanding what was going on, Brian's heart sank within his chest. Heartbroken, confused and angry, he turned in haste to walk out of the diner. Distracted and not completely aware, he collided with a newspaper stand. Michele reacted to the commotion and turned towards the sound. She instantly noticed Brian moving towards the door and leaped to her feet, rapidly trailing after him.

"Brian, wait!" Michele caught him in the middle of the street. Feeling her hand on his shoulder, he stopped and turned to speak with her. She noticed his eyes intense and red, his face flushed with mixed emotions of hurt and anger. Standing there looking at her, he was not sure what to say next, what to do now. Lost, angry and deeply confused, Brian was scared of what Michele was going to say next.

Someone finally spoke. Brian asked, "What is going on? I thought we had something." He partially turned to walk away. "I can't deal with this now. I really thought we had something."

Michele tried to explain, but much went unheard. Emotional herself, the words didn't come out clearly. "I did not know he was coming," she explained. "He mentioned seeing me again months ago, but I never figured he would just show up. I did not take him seriously." Her eyes filled with tears. "I told him NO. I'm glad now because I told him we are done, forever."

In the emotional confusion, Brian only heard her say she was glad he came. Those words ripped at his soul. Could he have been so wrong? Brian knew at this point in time he simply couldn't make sense of it all.

"Michele, I have to go. I have to run this race in three days. I can't deal with this now. If I see you again, at the finish line, we will work it out. If not, I'll know I was wrong. I'll understand." His voice broke.

With that, they parted. Neither sure of where they stood. Michele thought she just told Brian that she wanted to be with him. She thought she explained that the only reason she had dinner with her former husband was to end his hopes that there might be a future. She wanted to tell Brian that it took every ounce of her strength to be in the same room with him and that when he reached for her hand it made her skin crawl. She wanted to explain that she only wanted to be in his arms and that she felt safe with him. In the confusion and emotional energy, much went unsaid. In a blink of an eye, Brian's planned homecoming, an event that he thought would be the turning point in their relationship, laid broken in the middle of the road.

Heartbroken, Brian spent the next two days keeping his mind busy. Michele called and she texted. Reading her words, in clear text, the story became clear. He felt terrible for the misunderstanding. He was sorry he did not trust her more, but so much was new and undefined. His heart was broken over the misunderstanding.

Michele likewise only wanted to fix things, there were no hard feelings, she understood how things may have looked. She also knew she loved him.

Brian called her. "I am sorry I reacted the way I did. It's all me. I had big plans and they went off-course. I understand now. I'm sorry I was so hurt. You did not invite him or expect him, I believe you. You're busy and I have to focus. I have to make sure I'm right mentally. I'll see you at the finish? We can pick right up where we ended. If you decide not to be there I understand too. But know for certain I care for you; just let me run this race."

Michele answered, "I will be there. I promise and understand. You run this race. Brian, do good for Hanna, for you, and for Abby. She believed in you as I do and I will be there."

Brian stared out the window of his camper. Outside of recovering emotionally, he had two major tasks to accomplish.

CHAPTER 13

Task at Hand

In an attempt to not get overcome with the unknown of his relationship with Michele, Brian concentrated on the known. The known was the notorious challenge of running 100 miles. The only way he could keep his thoughts focused was to concentrate on the two most formidable tasks. The first since he was running this race unsupported, was to develop a plan that would take maximum advantage of the Aid Stations provided at the race. Second, he needed to ensure all his race gear was identified, lined up and ready for action. For Brian, the next two days would be as taxing mentally as the physical ascent up Hope Pass.

The attempt to run the Leadville Trail 100 is demanding in its own right. Running this classically rugged endurance test without a support crew magnified the task. Brian planned to do just that. Running the event "un-crewed" meant receiving no outside help other than what the race provided in the line of food, first aid, and hydration. Everything else that may be needed, such as dry socks, medicine, sunscreen or extra gear, would have to be carried by the runner. The majority of those who take on the 100-mile race have crews who ferry support items along the course. The crews also provide motivational and emotional support when the challenge gets hard and the bottom may be falling out. Brian would be facing the Leadville Trail as he had faced much of his life: alone. There would be no support system, no safety net, only the hope of a smiling face at the end of his journey.

To nearly everyone else, running 100 miles over 30 hours without sleep was enough of a challenge. Brian desired the extra sense of adventure that running solo provided. When he pitched the idea to his editors they agreed. There had been plenty of Leadville coverage from the viewpoint of those with crew support, vehicles, pacers, and, in some cases, complete operations dedicated to the care and feeding of the runner. A written article covering the daunted Leadville Trail 100 from the voice of a solo runner may have never been captured before. Everyone agreed he was the man for the job. Hidden in the mountains was another purpose.

Inside his home on wheels, a full-length trail map was tacked up on one of the walls. On this, Brian traced out the course with notations for the Aid Stations, elevation, terrain and water crossings. He reviewed all of this information along with details of every hill, every mile and key points along the course. Broken into segments, each leg of the race began and ended at an Aid Station. Anything not carried in his racing vest, a lightweight backpack, he planned to acquire at these race-provided pit stops. It would be at these stops that he would have the opportunity to refuel and resupply. Brian knew taking maximum advantage of these spelled success or failure.

The second task at hand involved getting his race gear prepared and support items organized. This race would feature water crossings, mountain climbs, running in extreme heat conditions during the day and bone-chilling temperatures at night.

Brian had to ensure he had the right running gear available with his pack arranged in a fashion that took advantage of the "pit stops" along the way. Food items would be available at the Aid Stations, but fresh shoes, socks, and clothing were uniquely his to carry. Most important of all was carrying enough water to get to the next Aid Station. With two hand-held water bottles and two bottles attached to his race vest, it may be stretching it, but Brian felt he could make it.

Thursday – pre-race dinner

Normally as a big race approached his sleep pattern suffered. Brian did not suffer like so many of his fellow runners from dreams of arriving late to the starting time. He also did not endure dreams of being a victim of some horrific injury, getting lost, meeting up with an angry grizzly bear or forgetting a most important piece of race gear. What disturbed his sleep cycle the night before a race was the uncontrolled impulse to make up every hour on the hour to check to see what time it was. Oddly enough during the days leading up to Leadville, he hardly tossed or turned.

Brian viewed the night before the eve of a race as the most important night for rest. He slept well throughout the night. Hanna likewise never opened her eyes. Once giving in to the start of a new day, excitement coursed thru his veins. Today was packet pick up and medical check-in day. Up to this point, all of his training had been for an event yet to come. For a far off goal, today would be the first official function of the Leadville Trail 100 Mile race and he was very excited.

Packet pick up began at 11 a.m. Brian decided to go a bit later so he could coordinate picking up his race number and medical check-in with attending the Thursday night carbo-loading meal which would kick off at 5 p.m.

Although a small race compared to the big city mega marathons that Brian had covered, the atmosphere at packet pick was contagious. Walking up to the table to begin his first official action as a Leadville racer Brian introduced himself to the volunteer who took his I.D. card and scanned an entry list for his name. He always got nervous during this process no matter the size of the race. For some unexplained reason, he always feared that somehow his name would not be on the official race entry list.

The girl looked up from the table and paused. "I don't see your name here?"

Brian lost his breath. "Are you sure, it's spelled B R I A N" he paused for just a second.

"Oh wait, not with a Y an I." The girl again scanned over the roll call of names. "I see it right here. I'm so sorry for the confusion."

Oxygen once again filled his lungs. Brian was relieved when the volunteer took the cap off her yellow highlighter and drew a highlighted line over his name and called out his number.

"Number 2 7 8 that's you, Brian, have a good race. I'll see you in Winfield, I'll be working the Aid Station there."

"You had me there," he chuckled. "I might need a week or two of recovery time from that cardiac episode."

It was on to medical check-in. Brian hoped he did not get disqualified because of high blood pressure.

Stepping up to the medical tent Brian again introduced himself, this time high-lightening that he spelled his name with an I. Nearly instantly an older gentleman found his name and asked him about his present state of health.

"I'm better than ever," Brian replied.

"That's good." The volunteer made a note on the registration form. Then he went on to explain the medical guidelines for competing in the race. "At the medical Aid Stations, you'll have your pulse and weight taken." He further explained that the staff "will be looking for signs of severe fatigue and weight loss. If you drop more than 7% of your body weight, you may be pulled from the race. If your weight is down between 3%-5%, you may be retained and asked to get some food and water into you to bring your weight back up." And with a serious tone, looking Brian right in the eyes, "Our medical staff members are looking out for your best interests and they have the authority to pull you from the race if they feel your health is in jeopardy or that your mental ability to make good, safe, decisions is compromised." He went on again to stress "THEIR DECISIONS ARE FINAL."

Brian nodded and confirmed he understood, "I respect that, I want to finish this race very badly, but I want to live another day even more. Thank you for what you do and thank your medical staff for me."

Brian walked away from the medical check-in with a yellow medical wristband around his wrist. Packet pick up was done, now Brian felt like a real Leadville athlete.

Yearly at the Leadville gatherings, a diverse mixture of athletes came together. The experienced professionals included the likes of Scott Jurek, Hal Koerner, Anton Krupicka and Marshall Ulrich, each one an ultra marathon champion in their own right. The majority of the starting line-up was made up of the middle-of-the-pack veterans. Then you had the Leadville rookies. You could pick them out at first glance. This sea of ultra runner humanity was all packed into the crowded accommodations for the same purpose. To run 100 miles. Brian thought it rang true to the spirit and character of the ultramarathon sport, that at an event like Leadville, you would see the best of the best hanging out and dining with a rookie class of unproven talent.

Although a rookie himself, Brian felt comfortable in the surroundings. He was an accomplished endurance athlete, after all. On his resume were a number of long distance and challenging trail runs. Running 100 miles was a challenge, but it was not "the" test behind this race. If he wanted to simply run 100 miles there were plenty of events that ensured success. The right venue, with a smaller, less-experienced and talented crowd, he just might threaten to place high in the standing. Leadville was different. The town was distinctive. The people who lived there were unlike most. The throng of runners who signed up to tackle this event were likewise not typical. Each year some of the world's best ultra marathoners participated here and each had their own story as to why. Brian was very much at home among this group.

After the welcoming and some encouraging words from the race director, Brian carried an overflowing plate to a table with two other runners already seated. The runner nearest him on the same side of the table was a slim male maybe a few years older. Across the table was a middle-aged woman, wearing a Leadville shirt from 2007.

Before sitting down, he started up an exchange.

"Hi, my name is Brian, this is my first time here. Can we share a table?"

The guy sitting next to him looked up from his plate of spaghetti, extended his hand and in a strong Texan accent, addressed Brian back.

"Howdy, I'm Blake from North Texas, a rookie as well."

The woman spoke up next. She was a petite blonde with a Scottish accent and a cheerful smile.

"I'm Ally from Virginia Beach…and since we are declaring our Leadville resumes, I'm a three-time finisher. Brian, you're no rookie, come on, I've read your features in *Trail Running and Beyond.*"

"Thanks, my cover is blown now" Brian shyly replied back. "This is my first Leadville and I'm going solo. I sure feel like a rookie."

"Oh, crap," the Texan with blue eyes and a muscular build for a long distance runner replied between bites of noodles. "That statement sure makes me feel like a wimp. My luck, here I sit with a three-time finisher and a solo runner. Good to meet you guys."

Ally replied, "Nothing like going big the first time up in the Rockies. Good luck with that, Brian."

"Have a seat," Blake offered up.

After this brief exchange, Brian sat down and offered a silent prayer. In the middle of a room full of well-conditioned athletes, he had one more moment to reflect on where he was and what was about to take place.

Scanning the room there came a moment, when a tall thin girl, who looked very athletic walked by. Instantly she acquired Brian's attention and not for her long legs, brunette hair or stunning looks. What garnered his attention was that he had caught a glimpse of her Leadville sub 25-hour buckle that hung low around her waist.

Born out of the traditional rodeo belt buckle won by champion bull riders, most century distance ultra marathons adopted the same tradition of awarding buckles. Calling back to western heritage, the race winners buckle was much larger and grander than those awarded for completing the race. Some events also awarded special buckles for runners completing the course in certain time frames or for running the race unsupported.

At Leadville, all runners completing the race in under 25 hours would be awarded a gold and silver buckle. Finish in under 30 hours and you would receive a silver buckle. Running solo, he understood a sub-25 hour buckle was most likely out of the question. The primary goal was to be able to walk across the stage Sunday at high noon and receive a finisher buckle, no matter what his finishing time would be. Brian would be satisfied and consider this a successful race with a finishing time of 29 hours 59 minutes and 59 seconds earning a Leadville buckle of his own.

Hanging prominently inside his mobile apartment was the framed belt buckle from his first 100 Mile race. Brian's goal for that race was to simply finish. It was on lap seven that his pacers George and Ben confirmed the math that he was on target for a sub-24 hour finish. To this day when Brian reflected back on that race he could still feel the emotions of battling through those two final laps to complete the 100 Mile Endurance run at Umstead, NC. He completed that race in 22 hours 51 minutes and 5 seconds. It was with great pride and extreme emotions that he accepted the rectangular shaped bright silver buckle for a sub-24 hour finish from race director Blake Norwood.

As Brian watched the tall brunette walk away he could only hope to repeat that performance and meet his goals or even exceed them at Leadville.

The trio of runners conversed about past experiences and their expectations. During breaks in the conversation, Brian went to work on his dinner; six large pizza slices, five big chocolate chip cookies and a large bottle of water. One would think that would be all the calories and carbs he'd need to fuel his way to Hope Pass and beyond. Truth be told, this meal would be consumed as fuel a mere 15 to 20 miles into the race.

It was a fact that this was Brian's first 100-mile race at high altitude. Although he had no doubt about finishing a race of this length, Brian's only reservation was finishing with the additional burden of being self-supported. Along with the strain of running solo came the professional pressure of the deadline with his editors. A successful solo finish at Leadville would sell. A solo Leadville collapse would not…unless it was painfully spectacular and bloody. Either way, Brian truly wanted to avoid both of the latter options.

The pent-up energy and excitement inside the gym could be cut with the proverbial knife. All the conversations turned to the routine questions. Year after year, the majority of faces changed, but the questions always remained the same. "How many Leadville races have you run?" "What is your pacing plan?" "Who do you have on your support crew?" Brian chatted with some old friends and the few runners he had met while living in Leadville. Many asked about Michele. When he was asked about her, he liked hearing the sound of her name.

The Leadville dinner was in full effect. The 6th Street Gym was warm, stuffy and bursting at its seams. Although there was plenty to eat, some of the runners skipped this meal. Some were a bit superstitious about the traditional race provided meal. Many feared they would have a negative reaction to the food, the seasoning or the quality of the offerings. He never had these issues and often joked about having a cast iron stomach. Brian hammered away on the pizza slices with the same gusto he planned to attack Hope Pass.

FRIDAY – race briefing

One day out from the start of the race, the quiet mountain hamlet would become alive with activity. Brian slept in until after 8 o'clock. The camper was quiet as the morning sun beamed through the window shades. Hanna enjoyed the extra sleep as well. She did not get up until Brian rolled out of bed, dressed and began making noise.

This morning, Brian prepared to go for a very short run. The three-day break from running was starting to give him the jitters. He knew the downtime was required, but he itched to hit the trails. Part of his life, a life he grew accustomed to was missing. Today's effort would not break any records. Its function was only to prove that his legs were still functional. After letting Hanna out and tossing one of her toys around a few times, he gave her a big hug as he put her safe and sound back inside the camper. Brian closed the door, ensured it was locked then turned and took off. Although his legs would do the majority of work, they were not the only thing that needed a working over.

Once back at camp, it was time for some camp-style waffles and scrambled eggs. Hanna always loved it when they had waffles. They were her favorite, although she did not get any of the maple syrup. She loved the sweet taste but it made her beard sticky. After breakfast, it was time to head into town and attend the race briefing. The trip into town was a short one, one he had made many times.

Nearing the intersection that would take him to the final race brief, his thoughts were distracted and his mind wandered. He day-dreamed about Michele as he walked the now empty roads. With new reassurance, Brian believed he understood where their relationship stood. Yet something still bothered him. He remembered Michele saying that her former husband had come to Leadville on his own accord. She repeatedly said she did not want him there, that she did not invite him. Brian's mind was conflicted; he questioned how many men would fly halfway around the world without a bit of encouragement. It was a question he still had to resolve with himself, if not with Michele.

The gymnasium was again packed with runners and crew. A day before many gathered here to fill their bellies. Today they came to fill their minds. Here the official race briefing with up-to-date trail and race conditions would be given. Any changes in race rules or procedures and last-minute instructions would be given out to the entire field. All race entrants were required to attend. In the cramped gym, Brian paused to reflect at the gathering of such running talent.

Race Founder, Ken Chlouber, a man cut from the very fabric of the heritage of Leadville, stood in front of the gathered crowd. In 1982, as the town struggled with the downsizing of the mining industry. Chlouber, an out of work miner himself, had an idea that would put his town on the map again. He proposed to host a 100-mile footrace through the high mountains. Most residents including local medical professionals thought he was crazy and voiced concern over such an extreme endurance event.

"You're going to kill someone," some in the community warned when he first presented his plan.

Ken reasoned "Well, then we *will* be famous, won't we?" After the first successful race was held with no fatalities, the Leadville race series was born.

Standing tall in his trademark weathered cowboy boots, blue jeans, black button down shirt and stunning black cowboy hat, his appearance was that of a rugged mine worker chiseled from the very mountains that he had made his living from for the majority of his life. Unmistakably noticeable around Ken's waist was a hubcap sized Leadville buckle. Chlouber an avid marathoner and endurance athlete himself stood in front of the masses with a great big western smile. Ken took a few seconds to scan the crowd then he announced, "All you Leadville runners, you are family. We understand what got you here, the work, the miles, the pain and the financial commitment. You will always be our family."

Brian had heard tales of the big personality that was Ken Chlouber and with those words, the hair on the back of his neck stood up and chills ran down his arms. If he survived the race, Brian had a plan to ask Ken for a one-on-one interview. Today he simply sat in awe of the Leadville legend transfixed on his every word.

Ken cleared his throat and began to share his twenty plus years of Leadville race experience. Chlouber started off by saying that success at

Leadville hinged on "the ability to get more out of yourself than you ever thought possible." He further explained what it took to continue when most others would quit, "to go on when others would turn back." In front of the race crowd, Ken held up a silver buckle. From Brian's vantage point the metallic object was barely visible, but instantly he knew what it was.

"This buckle and this motivational speech," Ken paused, "will only last you until you throw up for the first time. As you throw up on the side of the trail there will go your motivation, there will go your desire for a shiny buckle. You have got to want to finish this race for some other calling." Those words hung in Brian's soul, he turned his head to the ceiling and stared at a spot on the weathered tiles of the gymnasium. For a moment he was no longer in the over packed 6th Street Gym, Brian was alone and at a turning point in his life.

The crackle of the public address system brought him back to his senses, and he hoped he did not miss out on any important information.

Ken continued, "You are better than you think you are and you can do more than you think you can." Those words resonated in the room as Chlouber continued to talk about the race.

To close the night Ken asked every runner to give their personal commitment to never give up on their dream. "The pain will only last 30 hours if you quit the pain will live with you forever." The room grew quiet. "Will you commit to finish? "he asked the assembled mass.

The crowd of gathered runners sang out. Some responded by yelling "Yes!" Others simply clapped and some whooped and others hollered. The response was loud, but not up to Ken's standards. He then asked everyone to stand and repeat his mantra "I COMMIT I WILL NOT QUIT!,"

Ken called out, "With gusto this time, from your heart, your mind and from your SOUL. I COMMIT I WILL NOT QUIT." Every runner in the gym stood and echoed Ken's statement this time with a thunderous volume.

I COMMIT I WILL NOT QUIT." They responded loudly enough to satisfy Ken and his staff.

"Okay, I'll see you at the start and we will be there at the finish line where your life will be forever changed.

Before departing, Brian snagged a few more cookies and headed out the door. Walking alone, he looked up towards the trail, then down the street. Brian was reminded that his battle was just about to begin.

As Brian walked alone on his way back to the campground, a person with a nondescript figure from the other side of the road yelled out in jest, "Glad I'm not you tomorrow!"

Brian thought about it for a moment. He paused at the meaning of those words. All the miles run in the early hours of the morning. All the training runs that he ran in cold, wet and windy conditions, the pain and suffering, both physically and emotionally all lead him to this point in time. Here he was, the shy little boy that no one thought would amount to much. The misunderstood young man that no one really embraced, save Abby. Here he was standing in the middle of an often forgotten and misunderstood mountain town about to run one of the toughest races in the nation. Brian paused and considered what the shadowy person in the distance had said. Slowly he turned in the direction of the lone figure and gave a cheerful wave.

Before the silhouette of a figure could get too far away, Brian called out "Honestly, I would not want to be anyone else. I've trained hard for this...I will finish."

"Then have a good race, God Bless, and good luck." The voice answered back.

Brian continued home.

CHAPTER 14

Leadville Trail 100 - The Start

Leadville to May Queen Aid Station

The start of any extreme endurance race is emotional. At Leadville, where 700+ runners tackle one of the most challenging races in the United States, the atmosphere is electric. The emotions were only dwarfed by the 12,600-foot peak known as Hope Pass. This morning would be no different.

Securing a ride to town from an employee of the campground, Brian arrived a solid 45 minutes prior to the 4 a.m. race start time. On race morning he was normally one of the first to show up. Being the early bird was just one of the parts of his normal race routine. He enjoyed the quiet moments prior to every race where he could, be still, pray and get his mind focused. After arriving in town, Brian sat on the edge of the sidewalk along 6th Street just beyond the Start/Finish line. From this vantage point, he was able to take in all the happenings going on around him. At first, the area was quiet; only a few runners were out milling around. It was not long before the crowd started to find their way onto the street. Rapidly the atmosphere changed as he was joined by numerous other Leadville hopefuls. In the following moments, he would begin the toughest race of his life. Brian understood that his body would be subjected to a form of extreme physical effort and stress far beyond anything he had faced before. He accepted that life for the next 30 hours would be painful.

It was still dark as the crowd gathered. The sun had yet to make an appearance over the eastern skyline. The race officials called for the field of runners to line up for the start of the race. With these words, his pulse rate quickened as he made his way to a position in the middle of the starting pack. Brian soon found a comfortable piece of real estate amongst the growing crowd.

Out of character, Brian spoke up out loud as he looked up into the still dark sky. Speaking to no one in particular, but also to everyone within an earshot, "Today is Leadville Day," his voice called out.

A neighbor softly spoke back, "Well this is it. You ready?"

Without a verbal comeback, Brian motioned his eagerness to get going with a high-five and a big smile. The meaning was understood by all around them.

Then for a moment, Brian paused to reflect on just where he was. This was the day he had set his sights on since leaving his family, Abby's family, and his hometown behind him. This was the race he told Abby about when they first talked about his goals as a runner and a writer. Abby knew this challenge meant the world to him. She always supported him. Today, Brian knew, this was going to be the moment he would reclaim his future.

Looking around the starting line near the corner of 6th and Harrison, he marveled at the scene. Hundreds of runners all decked out in different, yet surprisingly similar high-tech running gear. Some braved the cold and wore shorts. Some wore running pants or tights with a mixture of long, and short-sleeve shirts. There were those, like Brian, with backpacks secured behind them. Others carried only a water bottle or hiking poles.

Brian was wearing a black cap with a white embroidered logo from his first ultra race, The 24 Hour Ultra Run Against Cancer in Hampton Roads, Virginia. Above the bill of this cap was a pair of sunglasses positioned at the ready for later on when the sun would appear and threaten to fry his skin like so much bacon. He also wore a long sleeved orange shirt, a race vest that doubled as a mini high-tech lite weight backpack and a pair of full-length black compression tights under a pair of four-pocket shorts in the same color. Last, but not least were his favorite running shoes. They were bright orange and topped by a black pair of gaiters designed to keep the small stones and dirt out of the shoes. The gaiters, black with little white dog prints, he wore as a tribute to Hanna and every dog that kept him sane throughout his childhood. When people questioned him on his selection of prints, Brian told everyone that Hanna purchased them for him.

One thing common to everyone this morning was the lighting equipment. Nearly every runner starting the race had a headlamp secured by an elastic headband around their forehead or carried some type of flashlight in their hands. Brian had both. If someone did not know that this was the beginning of an ultra endurance race, they may have thought it was more likely to have been an alien invasion zone. High-powered headlamps beamed piercing rays of light onto the ground and into the still dark morning sky. For the outsider, it was surely a sight to see.

Brian looked around at all the faces in the crowd and in them he saw some common expressions. He saw nervousness. He saw wonder and confidence. He saw fear. He wondered what his expression might look like to his fellow competitors. As he scanned the crowd, few faces looked familiar. He smiled, waved and wished them good luck and good running then turned politely in the other direction. The majority of the crowd had their game faces on.

At one point, he thought he may have seen Michele walking along the sidewalk. Was that the familiar profile of her face? Maybe she was looking for him, he reasoned. Brian tried to move in her direction, he thought that if could just get a little closer look he might know for sure if that was her. The press of the crowd of runners surrounding him made that impossible. Unfortunately, as fast as he had noticed her, the sea of humanity took over any chance of knowing for certain. He became frustrated and sensed his heart rate begin to climb. This caused him some alarm. Brian knew the only thing that needed to be on his mind was this race, his plan and the mountainous terrain that lay out in front of him.

The buzz of the PA system caught everyone's attention. The nervous crowd grew quiet. All the side conversations, all the jitters stopped. The crowd seemed to come together as one. They all seemed to focus their attention as the morning race announcements were given. Once all the information had been updated, next came the national anthem. As a local volunteer sang, the collective group of runners began to retreat into their own personal zone.

As the song came to an end and in the final minutes of calm before the storm, Brian, simply took one more moment to look around. He waited a long time to get to this place and he wanted to ensure he would remember it well. As he scanned the scene around him Brian took notice of the field of runners surrounding him. He noted that some looked determined and ready to prove themselves. Brian also noticed some had the jitters; they seemed unable to stand still. There were the groups that made small talk; they found comfort in getting to know everyone around them. Then there was the group he fit into; they were lost in a quiet moment of prayer and reflection. He lowered his head and with eyes closed, "Dear Lord God, only you know the state of my heart and mind. Only you know the abilities of my body. Please guide me today and settle my heart, show me where Michele and I should go and tell Abby I love her. I can do all things in you. In Jesus name, I pray. Amen."

As quickly as that quiet moment set upon him, it was gone. A countdown followed, four....three...two..one. A single dull gunshot blast went off and although he knew it was coming, it still managed to startle his senses.

From where he was positioned he could not see the starting line festivities. Standing about midway in the pack he simply heard the gunshot blast. Above the backlit banner hoisted over the starting line, a mushroomed cloud of the light gray emissions exit the barrel of the gun and cut into the early morning sky. Then he thought he heard someone say "GO!" Before another thought could enter his mind, they were off. With the slow and eradicate rush of the crowd, it took a few minutes to make his way across the starting/timing mats. Once under his own power, Brian slowly made his way down 6th Street. Not a quarter mile from the starting line Brian pulled up and stopped dead in his tracks.

Many of the witnesses standing on the sidewalk must have wondered if he was injured, they may have questioned what went so terribly wrong, so soon. Nothing was wrong, his mind and body were fine and ready for the challenge. Before leaving town a beckoning within his heart called for him to stop along the side of the road. Once stopped he turned in the direction of where Michele lived. Before he made his way out of town, he felt a desire to say a few parting words to three important people in his life. Anyone standing close enough would have heard him say. "Abby, I hope you're proud of me. I miss you. Hanna dog, see you soon, play nice with your doggie sitter" Brian had to pause to regain his composure. A lump formed in his throat. "Michele, I'll be back. We have too much to give each other." In more ways than one, the biggest day of his life had just begun.

Just as fast, Brian was running again quickly regaining his normal gait. The first five or six miles passed relatively quickly. It was nice to finally feel the trail beneath his feet. The smell of fresh mountain air sharpened his senses. Undeniably it was also invigorating to get into race mode. These first miles were very familiar as they would take him past the campground that he had been calling home. The temperature was cool, and crisp, but not cold. The pack of 10 or 12 elite runners had already separated themselves as Brian and several hundred other mid-pack contenders were beginning to find their collective groove.

The morning delivered nearly perfect running weather. The first challenging section of the race was a short, steep, rocky slope known as

Mini-Power Line. Here nearly everyone except those trying to win the event, walked the inclines. This early in the race most runners wanted to conserve their legs for the later stages. Brian followed suit and dropped down to a lower gear to power walk this section. This first segment of trails took the runners towards and around Turquoise Lake Road.

Brian settled into a conservative run/walk plan. He found himself paired up with a group of runners who were keeping near the same pace. Within this group were a couple Leadville veterans and a few rookies. Brian enjoyed the conversations and figured the group's energy would pull him along. He decided to stick with them at least until the May Queen Aid Station. The group quickly reached and crossed a boat ramp, then continued on the trail around Turquoise Lake towards May Queen.

Under the cover of the early morning darkness, the group, with Brian in tow, made their way along the edge of the lake. The view ahead was entertaining. A continuous chain of runners each one broadcasted a brilliant beam of light out in front of them as they ran. Brian chuckled out loud "The trail ahead looks like a mile-long centipede that got tangled up in some Christmas lights." He heard a few laughs out in front of him. Although it was an easier section of the trail, one wrong foot placement and your day could end quickly. Having memorized nearly every detail of this trail, Brian knew the darkness combined with a trail that ran very close to the water's edge could result in a runner getting wet in a hurry.

Brian and his adopted running group arrived at the May Queen Aid Station, the first oasis of the race in good spirits. Here the majority of runners linked up with their support crews. For the solo runners, these pit stops were vital occasions to refuel and refresh. They also provided a revitalizing shot of energy when the runners reconnected with the regular world. After only a couple of hours on the trail, Brian hung around just long enough to top off his water supply, a mixture of Gatorade and energy gels, then to grab a quick snack. Maximizing as much he could, he stashed a few extra snacks in the front pockets of his pack. It was a bonus that they had Reese's Peanut Butter Cups. That snack would be "a little spot of sunshine for later on," he told himself while he walked out of the aid tent. Surprisingly at this early stage in the race, some runners took the time to sit and rest. Comparatively, Brian was in and out very quickly. Back out on the trail, it was easy to link up with another group. The Aid Station at May Queen ended the first half marathon of the race.

May Queen to Fish Hatchery Aid Station

Leaving May Queen, Brian noticed the sun was beginning to crest. The daylight painted a wonderful hue of orange and pink in the heavens. A veteran in his new group warned those around him to not get so lost in the race as to forget the experience. Brian paused to take a quick picture then it was back to work. This part of the trail consisted of the first significant climb, approximately 11,000 feet, to the top of Sugarloaf Pass. With the beginning of a new day, one thought overcame him. "I'm running Leadville," Brian commented partially out loud.

Although focused on the race, Brian wanted to be sure he took some time to enjoy the experience. One of the other runners in this group overheard him and replied back, "I hear you there, isn't it great?"

Some of the runners in this pack were chatty. "Where are you from?" one would comment. "How many times have you run Leadville?" Another questioned the group around them. Others, like Brian, were more focused and in their running zone. Brian's mind was also back in Leadville. He noticed the further he ran away from town, the more his attention turned to Michele. He caught himself wondering where she was and what she was doing. After summiting Sugarloaf Pass, Brian would be faced with a steep and nasty descent.

After he cautiously, but rapidly pounded his way down Sugarloaf Pass, the next Aid Station was at the Fish Hatchery. With 24 miles down in 4 hours and 30 minutes, Brian navigated his way in and out of the Aid Station without much delay. As he made his way through the support zone he remembered a saying his running mentor George had told him during his preparation for his first 100-mile race at Umstead State Park in Raleigh/Durham, North Carolina. George a veteran of nearly 100 ultra marathons warned, "Beware of the chairs." The numerous chairs encountered at the various Aid Stations were to anyone competing against the clock contraptions designed to work against success. Each chair although looking comfortable was really able to tax energy and time during long races. George told him "the chairs look inviting, one would think a minute here or there would not hurt your race against the clock. Once you sit down the first time, it gets easier and easier to get off your feet again and again. You have to keep moving. The more time off your feet, the more time it takes to get back out on the trail and moving towards your goal". Brian made sure he heeded George's advice and was back out on the course in short order.

Fish Hatchery to Half Pipe Aid Station

If any part of this mountainous race felt routine it was after leaving the Fish Hatchery Aid Station. He may have been riding on the remaining high from the start of the race, or maybe it was the energy gained from the volunteers. Whatever it was, the effort, if not easy, was at least very conservative to run this part of the course. Brian's legs felt light, powerful and the exertion to overcome the stream crossing and the undulating trail was not taxing. Not to call this section of the course flat; it offered two good climbs, but they were not Sugarloaf Pass and certainly not the monster that awaited him at Hope Pass.

Fish Hatchery to Half Pipe was one of the shorter sections of the race. When auto-pilot took over, Brian settled into a nice rhythm. Run. Breathe. Trail. Rocks. Open fields. Trees. Run. Breathe. Repeat. The running here came easy, so easy, that time went by almost unnoticed. Brian hardly paid much attention to the distances he was covering. It wasn't long before he arrived at Half Pipe Aid Station.

As before at May Queen, Brian did not come off the trail to meet up with a support crew. This did not go unnoticed by one of his new found trail running friends. "Are you running this solo?" he asked. Brian simply nodded, smiled and made his way to the tables that had the food items laying out on them. "You're a beast," Brian heard as he made his way through the Aid Station. At Half Pipe the routine was simple: keep moving, spend as little time chatting as possible, get what was needed and move on.

At these long distance/adventure races, the support offered by the Aid Station volunteers could make or break the day for any would-be finishers. This race-course challenged you with distance, simply running 100 miles was not easy. The course confronted you with elevation changes, runners would climb and descend 15,600 feet, with elevations ranging between 9,200–12,620 feet. Likewise, the event would oppose you with the sheer altitude, the start of the race began at 10,600 in the center of the nation's highest incorporated town. On top of that, the number of hours it would take to finish this event threw down the ultimate endurance gauntlet. Traditionally, since the first running of this race in 1983, less than fifty percent have finished in the allotted time.

The race winner would cover the course in just under 16 hours. The record time was established in 2005 by Matt Carpenter who ran a blistering 15 hours and 42 minutes starting at just before daylight and finishing with the sun still hanging in the sky. The majority of runners would not be aiming for a win. A large number of the starting field would be more concerned with making all the cutoff times and simply finishing the race.

Those unable to make designated checkpoints in the allotted time were either pulled from the race or turned back for their own safety. A cutoff time had been established at the Hopeless Aid Station. Hopeless was an Aid Station approximately 1,000 feet below the 12,600-foot crest of Hope Pass. All runners needed to make the outbound checkpoint by 4:15 pm. A runner unable to make this benchmark had little chance of making Winfield the 50-mile point in the required time. Those outbound runners unable to make Hopeless in the required time would be turned around to Twin Lakes. For some, the 30-hour event cut-off time would not be long enough.

The volunteer workers, the majority of them runners or family of runners themselves, provided excellent support. At each stop as the runners passed through, the volunteers took time to interact with each of them. The social interaction lifted the spirits of a runner who might be down on his or her luck. Everyone's goal was to provide a smooth transition through the stations without much of a delay. To someone who had spent hours worrying only about putting one foot in front of the other, the simplest of tasks could be overwhelming. The volunteers took such a mental load off the competitors by taking their water bottles, cleaning them out and placing them back in their hands once they were full again. This gave the solo runners like Brian one less task to worry about. With two free hands, he was able to chow down on some food items to top off the fuel tanks before going back out on the course. The next pit stop would be at Twin Lakes after a demanding ten-mile section.

Half Pipe to Twin Lakes Aid Station

Leaving Half Pipe Brian was feeling great physically. Mentally he sensed some uneasiness. His focus was wavering a bit. His mind wandered back to Leadville and to Michele. This distraction caused him to lose focus on the pace he was trying to maintain. During a 100-mile run, maintaining your pace is a critical factor to success. Going out too fast, running too hard at the wrong time has undone many a good runner. At this point in the day, maintaining the correct pace was what would put you into a finishing position. Running too hard or too fast could put you in the medical tent or on the wrong side of the cutoff sweeper. Brian knew if he continued to focus on getting back to see Michele, he was setting himself up for disappointment, disaster, and despair.

This anxiousness and jittery pace caused Brian's heart rate to increase. This extra drain on his energy levels would tax his reserves if he failed to get it under control. He knew he had to stay focused. Not yet at the half-way point of the race, it was a bad time for a plan to come undone. As with any extreme physical event, any weakness in the mental game, any shortcomings in your physical preparation or any demons of your past can make it easy and acceptable to quit. Most runners would tell you, and Brian agreed, it was far easier to mentally quit than to give up for a physical reason.

Another concern that surfaced during this transition was that his backpack felt heavier today than he remembered in training. His race vest/pack had places for two water bottles up front and small pockets for smaller items like his camera and power gels. In the back was a storage compartment. In this compartment, was extra gear to fight off the night-time cold. Packed away was a light-weight fleece top, a beanie, and gloves, two pairs of socks, some body glide for chafing/blisters and some Band-Aids. Going into the race solo, Brian knew he had to carry anything he may need over the course of the race. He also knew that the extra load would be a burden. One extra pound carried over 100 miles would soon work to deplete his energy levels.

The trail carved its way through a series of meadows then it opened up to a river crossing. This crossing, Brian remembered, was tricky to navigate, but would prove to be very refreshing. The river served as a natural ice bath. Many runners took advantage of the ice-cold water by sitting for a spell or by doing leg lunges in the stream. The goal was to get as much of their legs submerged in the crisp mountain water as possible. The few minutes it took to allow the crisp mountain water to really soak in did wonders for the stress building up in their legs.

Exiting the stream, Brian stopped and bent over. Reaching his hands into the fast moving stream he placed his hands together and in a rapid movement splashed a hand full of water onto his face and another into his hair. This shockingly cold glacial water returned some pop back into his step. It was also at this point that Brian noticed the intensity of the sun shining on his face. Over the course of the last 39.5 miles, daylight had slowly made her appearance. Now as the race really began to challenge him, he became fully aware of how concentrated the glare of the sun could be at this altitude.

The toughest ten miles of the race would require all the extra vigor he could muster. Forty miles of running and fast hiking had delivered him to the lowest section of the race, a small valley at the foot of what would be the monster of the Leadville 100. Eight hours and 15 minutes had come off the 30-hour clock as Brian stood at the foot of this Ice-Age masterpiece, created when two of the earth's tectonic plates shifted then collided with tremendous force. Standing at this once violent intersection, he marveled. "God, I love your artistry and wonder, But I've got to make my way up and over this thing…twice."

CHAPTER 15

Leadville Trail 100 - Hope Pass

Twin Lakes to Winfield

The battle to scale Hope Pass began at 9,200 feet above sea level. The lowest part of the course was nearly 1,000 feet lower in elevation than the town of Leadville. With hours of physical effort to get to this point behind him, the real fight was now squarely in his hands. With the exception of the brief jittery period, he had won the battles presented before him and was in a good position to win the war. As confident as Brian felt, he knew the real campaign was just about to begin.

Leadville was a unique race for a number of reasons. The elevation, the terrain and the rustic nature of the town and the people who ran this race all came together in a perfect mixture to set this race apart from the other 100s. Another distinctive feature of the race was it's out and back course. Most 100 mile races were run point-to-point like Western States and Hardrock. Other notables as Umstead, Vermont, and Rocky Raccoon were run over looped courses. Not many 100s were run 50 miles out and 50 miles back. Fewer required competitors to face the most difficult climb on the course twice, the way that Leadville and Hope Pass necessitated.

As Brian began his first battle with the highest peak on the course he was faced with not only the climb but also with making space on the trail. At this point in the race, the trail up Hope Pass would be cluttered with those making their way up the summit. Some of these would be moving faster than Brian and some slower. The confined footpath would also be shared by the race leaders as they made their way back down the mountain. Seeing these elite runners as they passed by was both motivating and deflating all at the same time.

Observing these gifted athletes "race" down the hill, as they moved effortlessly over rocks, roots, and uneven terrain highlighted the separation between the average runner and world-class competitor. These elites had the gene, the R-gene. The Runners-Gene as Brian called it. The elite runners traveled at light speed down the trail compared to the middle of the pack runner as they made a deliberate and slow trek up. Yet as much as he enjoyed watching them run, witnessing their skills, it got frustrating to have to stop and pull off the trail to make way for them to pass. The trails up Hope Pass made for some tight running.

The climb to the summit started with a narrow trail cut through the tall pines. Switchback after switchback, step after step, with each laborious foot placement Brian advanced skyward. The elevation clicked upward like an altimeter of a runaway jet airliner racing toward the sky. Gone was any thought of running. Mental toughness aside, heaving lungs coupled with a heart rate that was nearing a catastrophic limit a fast hike was the best his body could muster. Climbing from just over 9,000 feet up through 10,000 feet, the fast hike turned into a fast walk. With nearly every step his arms pushed down on the top of his thighs, the extra force helping him advance forward and upward. Inside his heart raced and his breathing increased as his lungs struggled to supply enough oxygen to feed the muscles that were propelling his body forward. The only refuge during the ascent was the Aid Station at mile marker 45 so appropriately named Hopeless.

Arriving at Hopeless one first noticed this was a bare base of operations. There were no frills here. Competitors could get needed supplies to get over the top of Hope Pass and down to Winfield the half-way point in the race but not much more. There were no large aid tents, no flood lights, no congestion of support vehicles and no power. The volunteers who manned this outpost truly cared about supporting the runners. Small tents lined either side of the single wide trail that cut through the small compound. Unlike the previous stations where runners could link up with their support crews no such crew, team or family provided aid was available here. The only place for a runner to get off his feet was a few weathered old logs that were strung along either side of the trail. This was rustic camping at best. Then came the llamas.

Brian had truly never seen a llama before outside of a drive-thru zoo and a few crazy pictures on the internet. As he made his way into the camp, curiosity toward these strange looking creatures took over. There were white llamas with black spots, brown llamas with white spots and white ones with browns spots. Although still monitoring his time, he had to stop to snap a few pictures to capture this encounter. Who knew if he would even meet another llama, Brian reasoned with himself.

There was one particular llama who seemed not too impressed with Brian's actions or he was not well-socialized. Brian was not too sure after he tried to get into just the right position for a picture. When Brian had almost the perfect photo captured this one llama decided to shoo the human intruder away. As he hastily departed the scene, Brian thought he was spit at. As ornery as this llama may have been, they provided the only transportation to get supplies up the mountain. Brian asked one volunteer how many llamas they employed. He was told around 30. They may have been ornery, but they were as important to conducting the race as any support item.

Partially up the mountain, Brian needed the breather that Hopeless offered. The physical struggle to scale the mountain took a toll on his legs and lungs, but surprisingly what was beginning to challenge him was the sun. Of all the factors that Brian had accounted for in his intense planning, he did not account for the concentrated effects of the sun at the higher elevations. On legs that felt like overcooked noodles, he staggered into the Aid Station. Resisting the words of advice to keep moving, to not loiter, he finally sat on an open space on one of the logs and unplugged from the race for a few minutes. It was nice to stop moving.

Lost in a moment of rest and recovery, a volunteer snapped Brian back to reality when they approached him and offered to fill his water bottles. In that brief moment away from the trail, his legs regained some life in them. He thought about it a number of times, "A few more minutes would be great," but Brian knew he had to keep moving.

On the back side of this adventure, Brian knew there would come a time where he would have no choice but to park on the sidelines just to recover enough to continue. This early in the race he did not want to waste any time here. He did not want to burn valuable seconds or minutes he would need later. After he recovered his water bottles, he headed back onto the trail and back to work. Not wanting to give up more time to Hopeless or the llamas, he had to get moving. Leaving Hopeless he only hoped that the mean old projectile laden llama would be gone when he made his return trip.

The trails from Hopeless to the summit would be devoid of shelter. The narrow trail was now above the tree line. Gone was the shade the tall pines provided, gone was the wind break and gone was the cooling waters of the stream crossings. The competitors would have very little shelter from the weather if conditions turned ugly. There was no time to consider all this, for Brian it was time to get back to work and to continue the fight against the clock.

Back in the attack mode, the battle continued on the mountain against his personal drive and determination. Forward progress was the only acceptable outcome. No other thoughts, no other considerations, no other outcome was allowed to enter his mind. During the heat of battle a funny mantra resonated within his psyche, "Channel your inner mountain goat" Brian chuckled to no one in particular. Fighting on he reasoned to himself, "This war will be won by just one foot, just put one foot in front of the other." That little bit of self-imposed humor and focused determination helped to mentally push through the pain and strain of trying to get maximum effort out of his body in such oxygen-depleted conditions.

Scaling from 11,000 feet any semblance of controlled breathing went out the oxygen-deprived window. The grade at this section seemed to pick up a few percent as each foot advanced forward until reaching the final summit at 12,600 feet above sea level. The total elevation change of Hope Pass was over 3,000 feet in a little over five miles and Brian made it alive. Sure he was tired, beat up, his chest was heaving, but he was happy to have "the outbound section" of Hope Pass behind him. Standing on the summit, Brian finally stopped, looked around and took it all in.

On the top of Hope Pass Brian was speechless, partially because of the monstrous climb and partly because of the overwhelming beauty. His lungs burned. His heart pounded to the rhythm of a thousand drum-beats. His face and lips were sun and wind burned; he had survived the first encounter. Stepping to the side of the trail, he stared off into the distance with the tiny town of Leadville in view. As he stood there the seconds clicked off. With just over 11 hours into the race and a mere 45 miles down, Brian knew he had to continue moving forward. With one last glance at Leadville in the distance, he wondered what Michele was doing at that moment and then he thought of Abby. He took out his camera and snapped a few pictures, including one of himself. His last act on the top of Hope Pass was a silent prayer for Abby, her family and he asked God to provide a future with Michele. Brian then returned to the trail toward Winfield, Colorado.

The perilous descent into Winfield awaited. There would be no casual sightseeing while making his way down this trail. One failed foot placement and you could be face planted onto the trail, plunged down the rocky slope or worse, off the side of the mountain.

From past Leadville veterans, Brian had heard stories of treacherous falls on this downhill section. One such account haunted his planning and preparation for this section of the course. It happened to a past Leadville finisher during his sixth career decent.

No one was really sure what year it happened. The race day was near perfect, the seasoned runner was progressing well and nimbly making his way down from the summit when something went wrong. A toe caught or maybe his foot slide off a rock. His balance forfeited, an attempt to right himself resulted in a compromised foot placement. The side loading was too much, his ankle rolled, and then produced a terrible sound. Fellow runners around him would forever remember the sound and the cries of pain. The sounds were unlike anything they had ever heard before. It sounded like a small caliber gunshot, but it was the sound of a bone breaking. The sixty-year-old veteran fell to the ground and rolled violently. His nose, upper lip and forehead above his left eye bore the impact.

There were conflicting accounts of what happened after the fall. Did this unnamed runner survive? Did he finish? There were even tales of the runner turning down all medical care and finishing the race under his own power. Or was this just a tale grown to Hollywood portions which added to the legend of the race. Brian was unsure but knew he had to pay particular attention to every chosen landing spot and foot placement as he made his way down Hope Pass.

The trail down Hope Pass would last for approximately three miles, then would open up to a small dirt road leading into the near forgotten ghost town and the comforts of the Aid Station tent. Arriving here, those who still held onto the dream of finishing, had only to remind themselves, "I just have to do it all over again."

Winfield, Colorado, last populated in 1912, was a gold rush town founded by prospectors looking for a short-cut through the mountains. In its heyday, 1,500 people called this town home. Silver, not gold made the town famous in the past. Today the town and mines are mostly abandoned except a few remaining private cabins. Winfield was now a tourist spot where visitors came to see the old buildings and the town cemetery with the remains of 26 gravesites. During race weekend, Winfield would provide the turnaround point and Aid Station for a second date with Hope Pass. For some, Winfield would be the final resting place for their dreams.

The five miles from the Hope Pass summit to Winfield provide many with an opportunity to talk themselves into quitting. Winfield offered shelter. Winfield offered medical support. Winfield offered food and a place to rest. For the runner aided by supporting crews, Winfield offered their biggest disadvantage. For the crewed runner, Winfield offered them an easy place to call it a day. For the solo runner, there would be no one waiting at Winfield and this could be a major advantage.

After surviving the agonizing climb to Hope Pass and enduring the quad-pounding downhill to Winfield, many unfortunately, could not face the mountainous challenge again. Many simply could not muster the internal resolve, the self-motivation to once again head back out and take on the mountain for a second time.

Brian knew this transition area was a death trap. Crossing Hope Pass was brutal, crazy hard, and taxing on the mind and spirit. For some, both rookies and veterans alike, knowing they had to do it all over again could easily psyche themselves out. At the midway point in the race, Brian had been warned that he should not stop here for too long. Getting started again became exponentially harder the longer you stayed off your feet. Brian's eyes looked over the area; he saw defeat in the eyes of a few of his competitors. It scared him.

Brian made his way to the medical tent for the mandatory check-in. There, volunteer medical workers checked the runners in, recorded their weight and if they passed the quick medical scan, they were sent on to the resupply point. All of his vital signs checked out. Surprisingly, Brian had lost just over one and a half pounds. This was welcomed news as he was sure he made all his self-imposed nutrition checkpoints and was staying as hydrated as he could.

Brian took a beating physically that was for sure but, he was still mentally strong. He was determined to get in and more importantly out of Winfield as quickly as possible. If he did not linger, if he kept moving, quitting would never be an option. Sure, he knew the return climb was going to be demanding, but he was halfway done. His glass was half full. It had only been 12 hours and 30 minutes since the shotgun went off and now it was "time to get back to Leadville." With that statement, a new thought came over his being. "It's time to get back to living and loving." He paused at the foot of the trail that would take him back to Hope Pass. With a deep soul cleansing breath, he filled his lungs with the crisp rocky mountain air, then he breathed out, "I'm on my way." Brian left the ghost town with a renewed spirit, determined to make it over the top again, no matter what the mountain threw at him. The rest of his life waited for him 50 miles away and on the other side of Hope Pass.

Winfield to Twin Lakes

During every extreme distance run there comes a point when the body reaches its lowest state. There are times when athletes, even world-class athletes, who are performing at their best one moment, find that in the next second their world begins to disintegrate. The challenge is to ignore every natural instinct and continue to move forward. The survival instinct is built into each of us, the impulse that tells the brain to stop running in order to conserve energy for the vital functions. This natural stimulus is the one endurance athletes have to silence. The epic battle is to keep moving forward while every fiber of your being tells you to stop, to just stop moving. The secret to conquering this survival reflex is the ability to block out the whole and concentrate on the part. The part being, the next climb, the next Aid Station, the next switch-back, or simply the very next step. It was Brian's turn to struggle within himself.

It started on the second ascent up Hope Pass. Midway up the mountain Brian began to feel slightly light-headed, a bit unsettled in the stomach, and he began to develop a headache. At first, this little inconvenience did not slow his forward progress. A tool of the trade was the ability to block out any distress caused by pushing his body near or beyond its limits. Over the years he learned how to manage the pain away. When asked how he dealt with the dark times, his best answer was that he disowned the pain. He disowned the body part that was affecting him; it was no longer part of his anatomy or his plan. Setting this minor inconvenience aside, Brian kept his head down, his eyes focused on the trail and his willpower directed on the climb.

As he climbed higher up the trail a nasty case of nausea combined with the relentless grip of an ever-increasing headache. As hard as Brian battled to ignore his worsening condition, he began to lose the war. He tried desperately to keep moving, yet his head felt as if it was going to rupture like an over-ripe melon dropped on the floor. Adding to his deteriorating condition, his breathing became more and more labored. Then, the trifecta sent him into a potential spiral of defeat.

His pulse rate became a concern. He had never felt his heart beat so intently. The action of his heart was magnified tenfold over anything he had experienced before. He knew what it felt like to push his body to its breaking point. Brian also knew this was far beyond anything he had experienced, he became alarmed. It was hard to breathe. His body was struggling to keep up. His heart was working overtime within his chest cavity, yet he felt weak. He became dizzy. The sloshing in his stomach told him that his body was struggling to process the food consumed at Winfield. The result being that Brian's systems were failing to fuel the muscles needed to propel him up the tortuous climb.

The closer he came to his second summit, the more his body turned on itself. In this compromised state, he was sure he could deal with the pain or he could climb this mountain. He began to wonder if he could manage to do both. Something had to give, it turned out to be his stomach.

The headache and nausea got worse when Brian's stomach began to spin. Simultaneously his stomach did a few flip-flops followed with a few crazy gyrations. Then, a thousand feet short of the summit, Brian's insides did a violent twist and then a turn. His abdomen muscles contorted, then they seized tight. A sharp pain gripped his midsection like a vise gripping a piece of cold steel. He knew instantly what went down at Winfield was about to come up. For the first time in the hundreds of races on Brian's resume, he felt he was in real trouble.

In a panicked and dizzied state, Brian managed to step to the side of the trail, this allowed a few trailing runners to pass. Then the cramps got worse; it was all he could do to steady himself against a tree. "This is not good, I've got to get myself together," he vocalized out loud to no one in particular. He then attempted to place his head between his knees, but he lost control. His body began to revolt and all he was able to do was vomit. Brian's body did not simply rebel once, not twice, but at least three times. As he dropped to his knees, a few runners who passed by looked concerned.

Regaining some composure, Brian stood on the side of the trail. A few passing runners noticed the pale and feeble look on his face. A few were so concerned they asked if he was okay. Brian waved his hand, motioned that he was well and could handle this on his own. For a moment he simply stared off into the sky. His face bore a blank expression with no emotion; he thought for a brief moment he may just have been defeated. The thought of calling it a day entered his mind and it appealed to him. This was the second-lowest point of his life.

During this most compromised state, his brain played a trick on him. At his lowest, his thoughts returned to another more desperate point in his life. The morning after saying goodbye to Abby was not a day he chose to remember often.

The morning after Abby's funeral, Brian awoke feeling empty, alone and completely lost. His life seemed bleak. The world appeared very cold and dark to him. He was sure no good was left in the world or more close to home, his world. He never left his apartment that day. Brian simply did not have the strength to venture out into what remained of his life.

Friends and family called, some stopped by. Brian never paid them any attention. He ignored the phone and the knocks at the door. Lost in a black hole of his emotions, he sat inside alone with his grief and cried. He sobbed like a baby who had lost their favorite toy. He cried like someone who had been rejected. He wailed in anguish like a lost soul on the Day of Judgment and he wept like a man who had lost his will to live. This continued into the late hours of the night.

So lost in despair, so tormented with his condition, he nearly lost faith that there was a plan for his life. At some point, he cried out to God and to heaven: "Abby, what should I do? My life is not worth living without you!" He was sure, the neighbors heard him, but he didn't really care.

The answer he desperately wanted, almost as if Abby was talking to his inner soul, came to him. Brian could almost hear her soft voice. "Just keep living each day, for me. I promise you, life will get better." Brian continued to grieve until at some point he fell asleep.

A violent gut wrenching cramp deep in his stomach brought him back to reality. For a few brief seconds, quitting was a viable option. In what may have been just in the nick of time, Brian remembered what Steve, a friend, and Leadville veteran told him. "Continue moving forward, whatever you do, make forward progress, even when you're about to die." This rallying cry was just what he needed at the right point in time. As close to defeat as he was, if only able to keep up a slow death march or if even confined to a crawl, if he just kept moving forward there was still hope. As dreadful as it was, it could and most likely would get better.

"Just take that next step, simply put one foot in front of the other," he told himself. It was now a question of whether Brian's ravaged and compromised body would listen.

The first step was the hardest. Brian could not believe the amount of effort it took him to simply raise his foot and place it six, twelve and twenty-four inches in front of him. That movement led to another and another. Before long, a series of steps lead to a slight recovery. Over time this brought on an increased pace and tempo to his walk. His heart rate had lowered and although still labored his breathing was a far cry from where it had been. Brian went from a state of near exhaustion, from near collapse to being able to fast walk the remaining way up Hope Pass.

Reaching the top of the pass Brian did not take the time to admire the scene. He did not take the time to pose for pictures. He did not take the time to do anything. He modestly kept his head down and he kept moving. The battle with his stomach and ultimately his body made him well aware that he might just be fighting the clock before this race was over. After summiting, the descent passed like a blur. He could not remember the rapid downhill, Hopeless, or his second encounter with the Llamas. Brian only remembered walking into the Twin Lakes Aid Station for the second time.

When he arrived at the Aid Station, his energy levels were collapsing again. His pace had slowed, but his will to finish was solidly intact. Half-walking and half-stumbling, Brian made his way to the food tent to grab something warm to eat and something to drink. The noodles and chicken broth tasted great, they settled firmly in his stomach. His body was desperate for fuel. The climb back up the mountain, coupled with the pummeling descent, took a lot out of him. Desperate to get off his feet, Brian found an empty chair. He wasn't sure who it belonged to he just had to sit down. The structural integrity of the chair was tested as he collapsed into a heap. Brian surely looked like a defeated warrior.

An Aid Station volunteer noticed Brian sitting there. She approached and asked if he was okay, then congratulated him on making it this far. The answers he provided to her simple questions, were a bit off. Trained in how to recognize someone in a compromised state, his answers concerned her. "Hey Runner 278, I'm Rosie, a volunteer here at Twin Lakes. You're at mile 60 and some change, what is your name?"

At this point, he replied, "I'm not really sure." Although they both had a chuckle at his reply, this caused Rosie some concern.

"Well, Mr. I'm Not Really Sure, how about you sit here for a few minutes to allow your stomach to settle down and get some of our good food into you?" Rosie walked away. Looking back she further commented, "When you remember your name, give me a wave, I'll be right back over." Brian sat there staring off into some distant space. To an outsider, he must have surely looked beaten.

After five minutes, maybe it was 15, Brian was not sure, but Rosie reappeared with another cup of chicken broth and a cup of flat soda. She proceeded to tell him to take a small helping out of both cups. It was after the fifth spoonful of soup that he replied, "Rosie, I kind of think my name is Brian. Yeah, that's it, and I have a dog named Hanna. I really need to get moving to get back to her…she will be upset if I die up here."

Rosie looked at Brian in disbelief. Just moments before, she had entertained thoughts of having to pull him from the race and now he was cracking jokes. Rosie noticed the fire return to his eyes.

"What kind of dog is Hanna, Brian?" Rosie asked.

"A Miniature Schnauzer, she's going to be two soon."

"Brian, you give me 10 more minutes and you can keep on going. When you get home, give Hanna a big hug and a scratch behind the ears for me."

Twin Lakes to Half Pipe

Brian wasn't sure what was in the broth or the flat soda, but life was looking much better. After personally thanking Rosie for her help, he left the tent thanking the staff and high-fiving everyone within sight. Slowly he made his way back on the trail. Before he rejoined the battle, he paused to take account of just where he was in his quest. "I've got 30 some miles ahead of me." "Brian," he referred to himself in the third person. "It's time to fight for what you want."

With legs that screamed out in pain, muscles so exhausted that they had a hard time supporting himself, tendons so taut that they resisted movement and bones that ached to the core, Brian somehow convinced them all to once again moving forward. He called out, "See you later, Rosie!" With his energy levels on the upswing, a slow walk turned into a fast walk and a fast hike. It did not seem long before he was running, or maybe, it was more like a trot. The speed at which he was moving was not important, the fact that he was moving was. Making forward progress once again, Brian was on his way.

Once back on the trail, Brian felt a chill pass over his body. The setting sun brought along cooler temperatures. Outside of falling down among the jagged rocks and tumbling off the trail, the greatest hazard showed its ugly head once the sun set and dark hours set in. That danger was hypothermia. At this point, all but the elite competitors had settled into

163

some fashion of a walk/run routine. At this slower pace, some would find it hard to generate enough body heat during the night hours to keep warm. A veteran of many cold races, Brian was prepared for this.

Brian continued his trek forward while the sun likewise continued its decent on the horizon. As the temperature continued to drop, Brian knew it was time to mount his defense. Near a convenient fallen tree, he stopped alongside the trail. Brian sat down on a section of the tree that looked reasonably comfortable. Catching his breath for just a moment, slowly he slid off his combo race vest and backpack. Once free of the backpack he took out a light weight pair of black running pants and got ready to put them on. This all sounded like a good idea until he realized he had to take off his shoes to slip the pants over his feet. Such a simple task on any other day would go unnoticed, but today it would be a monumental battle.

His feet had taken a beating. Pulling off his shoes after the abuse they had suffered was a painful ordeal. After kicking numerous rocks and roots that laid in the trail, he could tell without seeing them that his toes were bruised and bloodied to the point that two of his toe-nails were barely hanging on. The tops and bottoms of both feet were tender. A few good-sized blisters were present on the soles of his feet. The most excruciating ones were between his toes. As much as it hurt, as much pain as he was going to inflict on himself, there was no question, he had to put on some cold weather gear or he might not make it through the night.

Removing his shoes was only part of the suffering. To get his feet into the pant legs Brian had to draw his legs up to his waist. This action involved muscle that had been overworked for the past 14 hours left the fiber of his muscles in cramped and tight knots. Such an easy task as putting on your pants today took a concentrated effort. Once his pants were on, Brian dusted off his socks. Next, he proceeded to clean all the debris out of his shoes. Then came the most painful part of the day; when he slid his feet back inside the torture devices that were his running shoes. That act left him wanting to scream out in pain and took his breath away.

Next, Brian pulled out his gloves, a beanie hat, and a fleece top. The gloves and hat he put to use right away. The top, he tied around his waist for later in the night. It was time to go back to work. Getting back on his feet was agonizing, but it had to be done. During the preceding miles, the onslaught of discomfort from his injuries was almost numbing. With a few minutes of reprieve, the pain that he had been able to tolerate became new again. With the weight of his body applied back onto his feet, his blisters caused rockets of fire to pass through every nerve in his body. As much as it hurt, he knew it was time to start moving. Resolve overcame the pain. Brian knew with each excruciating step forward he was closer to the next Aid Station and nearer to the end of this adventure.

Arriving at mile 69, Brian was in much better shape than when he got to Twin Lakes. Walking into the Aid Station he thought if it worked once, he would try it again. Taking up a seat along the wall, Brian fed himself another cup of broth and a cup of flat soda. He checked his watch and mumbled to himself "I'll give Rosie 10, no maybe like five minutes." With much-concentrated effort and ever-increasing pain, he got back up after the broth and soda were gone. Once on his feet, Brian hobbled by the food table, grabbed a few cookies and told the lady behind the table, "I have a dog named Hanna and she's waiting on me"

The lady looked at him oddly, but smiled and replied, "All right, hun, whatever it takes, you keep moving forward, you go get back to her."

CHAPTER 16

Leadville Trail 100 – The Finish

Half Pipe to Fish Hatchery

It was amazing how well Brian's body had restored itself. From the near disaster and resulting death march during his second ascent of Hope Pass to the recovery on his way to Half Pipe, Brian was moving well and in no real distress.

His body giving out on him was no longer the immediate threat. The next potentially grave challenge would be something the runners would have no control over. The trail and surrounding countryside were covered in complete darkness and the temperatures had fallen. Despite the best in cold weather gear if anyone stopped moving long enough, the body would not be able to produce enough internal heat to ward off hypothermia.

No matter how tired, Brian knew he had to keep moving. Without movement, there would be no heat. Without warmth, his core body temperature would drop. At this time of the night, at this stage of the race, if his body temperature dropped too far he would fall into the clutches of the insufferable cold and would have no chance of continuing. He settled into a run walk routine, where he ran the flat sections and/or downhill terrain and power-walked the hills. With so many miles on his body, it was all he could do and it worked. If he kept this forward movement up long enough he would find his way to the next Aid Station and some temporary relief. With enough repeated cycles, he would stay warm and survive the night.

At the Fish Hatchery Aid Station, mile 76 on the course, it was an opportunity to be out of the darkness and back among the living. There were times on the trail that Brian felt alone. When separated from other runners, his mind jokingly wondered if the world had ended and they simply forgot to call him off the course. The Aid Station offered a glimpse back at civilization. Brian returned to the same recovery routine that had worked so well since his return from near death atop Hope Pass. Gingerly sitting down, he gave himself a few minutes for his stomach to settle and then drank small helpings from a cup of soda and then some warm potato soup broth. Suddenly something alerted his senses. Something smelled good over on the other side of the tent.

A woman in a volunteer shirt noticed him looking her way. "Do you want some oatmeal?" she asked with a kind and cheerful voice. She walked his way.

"Oh, yes, please." Brian was so hungry he almost forgot about all the other pain coursing throughout his body.

With those simple words, a warm bowl was placed into his hands. She asked him, "You ready to get back to Leadville?"

"Yes, ma'am and thank you. The big climb is out of the way, now I just have to keep moving. I have to keep making progress. Plus, I have a dog named Hanna and I've met this girl I'm in love with, and I need to tell her."

With a comforting smile and a wink of her eyes, she turned and walked away.

The bowl felt good in his hands and the food felt more comforting in his stomach. As settling as it was to sit, to rest, to be still, he knew all good things would come to an end. Brian finished off the oatmeal then attempted to get back on his feet and back to the trail.

Paralleling a set of overtightened guitar strings that hinged on the verge of breaking, the back of his legs got his attention first. Standing upright, lightning bolts shot down the back of his legs as his hamstrings resisted. He wasn't so sure he could stand up completely straight. He must have appeared like the typical hunched over old man, but slowly and surely he was able to stand upright. Then he felt his lower back begin to spasm. His body was trying to resist, it wanted a few more minutes to relax. Truthfully, his body wanted to stop moving altogether. Although the longer he stayed still, the longer he remained motionless, the more of a challenge it was going to be to overcome the stiffness that had set in. It was time to move on or end his battle with the mountain right there. Nearly 21 hours into this adventure, the next leg of the journey was not going to be easy. The beastly return climb over Sugarloaf Pass was on the horizon.

Fish Hatchery to May Queen

Once back on the trail with the majority of the stiffness behind him, he was feeling unstoppable. Brian was also well aware that scaling the 11,000 foot Sugarloaf Pass was not a leisurely task. First, conquering this ascent for the second time would take a climb of 1,500 feet. The net effect on a tired and worn out body could be double that. Second, night time running was in full effect. And last, the trail was very unforgiving. Just when it looked like a runner was home free, Leadville offered up another test of your physical capacities. Brian was determined to keep moving and to pass this test.

To navigate this section of the course, one had to overcome a variety of trail surfaces. The surface was littered with rocks and stones that invited a twisted ankle, a broken leg or worse. There were miles of unleveled trails prone to snag a foot and leave you falling to the ground. If that was not enough, there were a number of "false summits" to test your mental toughness and emotional determination. With each summit, a desperate runner would believe they had reached the true summit only to be let down. Six or seven times, Brian had to overcome this mental test and push on to reach the top of the climb.

After summiting Sugarloaf Pass, Brian faced the long trek down to the final Aid Station. A final anything at this point in the race was emotionally uplifting. Although before he could see May Queen, Brian had a steady three-and-a-half mile downhill grade coming off Sugarloaf Pass. This section was historically painful and he wondered what damage the downhill would do on his already devastated quads. With every step forward, searing pain pulsated through the very fibers of his legs. Every time his thighs were used to break the effects of gravity, of running downhill, his muscles felt like fire burning through his flesh. To make it through the next step, Brian reminded himself constantly, the pain however intense would only be temporary. The pride of finishing this race would last forever.

He remembered Race Director Ken's words at the race briefing, "...failure will live with you forever."

At this point, nearing the end of the descent, nearing the beginning of the final chapter of the race, Brian knew if he just kept moving forward, if he simply made forward progress, if he blocked out the increasing agony a finish was nearly assured. For some, a finish was still in question.

After surviving his ordeal while scaling Hope Pass for the second time Brian had pretty much kept to himself. He did not interact with fellow runners, he did not run with a group like he had during the opening chapters of the race. Since the ugly mess some 20 miles behind him where his body nearly gave up alongside the trail, he kept his battles and his struggles to himself. He did not want to be a burden to anyone else. Little did he think he could be of assistance, a helping hand, or a race saver for anyone else.

Brian made his way down the precipitous trail that followed Sugarloaf Pass. Primarily, he focused all his available energies on selecting solid and secure foot placements. Second to that, he tried desperately to avoid any major rocks. His right big toe had suffered a number of head-on collisions, he was sure it was not up for another impact. With darkness covering the world around him, his attention was concentrated on the path in front of him which was illuminated by the beam of light projected from his headlamp. So focused to avoid the rocks and to ensure he did not trip and fall, he was not aware of much more around him.

Then something just slightly off the trail caught his attention. Seeing a fellow runner struggling was not new at this stage in the race. Over the last 20 miles, he had passed a hand full of runners in various stages of distress. There was the guy just outside the last Aid Station who took on a bit too much hydration and was vomiting uncontrollably. That scene brought back too many memories. Then strangely, he came across someone who decided to simply lay down and gaze at the stars. Now there was a runner along the side of the trail, but something looked different. Approaching, he was shocked when he discovered, a middle-aged female, standing alone and she was not moving. Brian sensed this time something was truly wrong, he wanted to help but he was unsure how to approach her.

He did not want to startle her or alarm her. To avoid a dramatic introduction, he moved slowly as he approached hoping that he would do nothing that would cause her to move rapidly because of his actions. He wanted to help, but also did not want to do anything that may have caused her to fall and hurt herself. Brian was also anxious that he may have come across a situation he was not equipped to handle. He questioned, was this runner in distress, was she ailing physically, emotionally, or had she lost her desire to continue, to run anymore. Brian approached tentatively. He walked up behind her slowly, cautiously and lightly made some coughing sounds like he was clearing his throat.

"Cough...cough. Are you okay" He asked very lightly in a tender tone so as not to startle her, but got no responses. His mind wondered and

171

began to panic as he looked at the women who was perfectly still on the side of the trail. She was upright, yet bent over with her hands on her knees. The bright beam of light from her headlamp was pointed directly at the ground in front of her. Silent and still she was making no movements and not responding in any fashion to Brian actions.

"Ma. Mama, are you okay," he attempted to make contact, louder this time. "My name is Brian, I'm here to help. Are you OKAY?" Brian raised his voice louder accenting his final words.

Something clicked, something caught her attention, almost if she snapped back to life. "Oh, I'm sorry. I'm okay I was asleep, at least I think I was asleep."

Her eyes looked dim and glassed over. Her voice was cracking, faint, and she sounded very weak. Brian tried not to shine his bright light in her eyes. The expression on her face looked confused and lost. When Brian noticed this, he became very concerned.

"As long as you're okay, we all need a good sleep." He tried to lighten the mood. "What's your name by the way? Were you really asleep?

"Yea, I was out., My name is Paula." The middle-aged women said. "I was running along feeling very tired when I thought I would step off the trail and stretch my legs. I thought for a second I would just close my eyes, then I heard you calling my name. How long was I asleep?" She inquired.

"I really have no idea, I've been here for maybe three minutes." Brian tried to fill in the time gap for her. "Are you going to be okay? Would you like to walk with me for a few minutes?"

"That would be nice," Paula replied. Her voice became stronger and Brian noticed her eyes looked clearer. This time they appeared to have some spark within them again.

"I've got a couple extra energy gels and some caffeine-laced gum if you would like some, you know to help give you a jolt" Brian laughed a little, Paula just smiled.

"Thank you very much, I think I'm good. I'm feeling much better now."

Ten minutes passed and the new found friends were making steady forward progress. Paula commented, "Brian, I'm feeling like a real person again so you don't have to hang out with me. I don't want to hold you back. The clock is ticking. You go ahead, pick up your pace and get back to running your race."

Still concerned Brian asked, "Are you sure?" He tried to look into her eyes again to get a gauge on how she was recovering.

"Yea, I'm good I feel so much better, Thank you very much, you pretty much saved my race. I think I've gotten my second wind...or maybe it's my fourth or fifth wind. It's been a really long race."

"No problem, you would have done the same for me...see you back in Leadville. Sunday morning. Right?" Brian tested her.

"You got it, Brian and thanks again," Paula said with a big smile as Brian picked up his gait, pulled away and proceeded to make his way back to May Queen.

Once down the steepest part of the climb, it was a two mile run on mostly unimproved roads, converging onto two bridge crossings separated only a short distance from one another. Brian had always enjoyed running across bridges. He especially enjoyed running over wooden bridges. His favorite were the old fashion wooden covered bridges that were found back east. There was something calming about crossing over a body of water and today Brian felt like he was crossing over to a new chapter in his life.

All that was left was a short run to the Turquoise Lake Road with a slight downhill grade into the May Queen Aid Station. At 86.5 miles, this would be the final Aid Station of the day.

It was hard for him to keep it all together. He was so close to finishing this race and so close to moving on. Walking into the aid tent, Brian found an open space along a wall and as much as it hurt, he sat down.

Before tending to his matters, Brian motioned for a volunteer to come over to him.

An older gentleman, who was tall and fit looking with almost white hair approached him. Brian noticed the volunteer was wearing the same JFK50 race t-shirt that he had. Partially out of breath he told the volunteer of Paula's situation and asked that they keep an eye out for her. "She was moving well when I pressed on." He stopped to catch his breath. "She told me she was okay. I just want you guys to be looking for her just in case." The volunteer gave him a pat on the back. Brian with a smile went back to inventorying his present state of affairs. Then he had one last comment, "I ran that race too. It's not easy!"

The volunteer turned around and smiled back at Brian, "neither is Leadville."

"Dang, you're telling me."

Brian sat along the wall staring at his feet. His shoes, gaiters, and socks were covered in trail dust. Underneath all these layers that were supposed to protect his feet his flesh burned. His lower legs hurt to the core; he wondered if you could bruise bone by running too much. The muscles in his legs were fried. His back hurt and his lungs just wanted a moment to catch up. Somehow in the middle of the crowded scene, the room went quiet, if just for a moment.

In the silence of his own mind, it hit him. *This race is almost over.* The impact of such a statement overwhelmed him. He sat nearly paralyzed as his eyes filled with tears. It was maybe 30 seconds or a minute at the most, but the noise of the tent returned and snapped Brian back into reality.

As good as it felt to be still, as much as his feet needed the time off, Brian knew he had to do something.

Slowly and painfully Brian stood up as every muscle in his body screamed out. Particularly in distress were his hamstrings. These long tendons were so tight he was sure they could be used to cut through glass. Steadying himself on less-than-secure legs, Brian held court with himself. "You're close, but this is not over yet. YOU have GOT to KEEP moving." From where he stood it was a short, but very long final half-marathon that separated victory from defeat and his dream of a Leadville Trail 100 Mile belt buckle.

He once again remembered Ken saying that the buckle could not be motivation enough. "Sorry Ken, I beg to differ, I WANT that buckle," Brian mentioned out loud as he gritted his teeth and coaxed his distressed body into moving again.

May Queen to Leadville

The trail around Turquoise Lake was monotonous, tedious and it meandered on and on and on. Or it just seemed that way. People would ask Brian what he thought about when he was running for hours on end. He normally had an easy answer: "I think about everything and nothing. I pray. I think about life in general. I think about MY life in particular, and I mostly dream." After nearly 24 hours on the Leadville trail, Brian was nearing the end of all the things he could or wanted to think about. What had an iron grip on his thoughts now was the pain, the pure exhaustion, the lack of sleep, and the overwhelming desire to just be done. Brian just wanted to be able to finish this race and move on with his life.

After all the miles, the mountainous climbs, the near-disaster ascending Hope Pass for the second time, the quad-pounding descent coming back down Sugarloaf Pass, the mental taxation of a trail that seemingly lasted forever, the race nearly had Brian's number. Here it was not a physical conflict as it was on Hope Pass. Instead, Brian was beginning to suffer emotionally.

The mental anguish of knowing you're so close, but so far, was tough to handle this late in the race. Deep inside his mental reserves, Brian held onto a mantra, a glimmer of hope that served him well in other tough races. "It is not the next mile, but the next step that is going to win the day for you." He trudged on and on and he concentrated on each step as a sign of victory. Small step after step, he eventually came off the trail and onto Turquoise Lake Road. It felt so good to have firm, level ground underneath him. Brian thought for a moment that this was the final road that would bring him to the finish line.

At this late stage of the race and sleep deprived, in all the twists and turns, combined with a lack of all ability to process critical thoughts, Brian had lost track of where he was on the course. His mind coaxed him to believe the solid footing of Turquoise Lake Road was really Sixth Street.

At the center of town and the place where this adventure began Sixth Street was also the street that would lead him to the finish line. It was uplifting to believe he was so close to the end and heartbreaking when Brian saw the pink trail marker that directed him back onto the trail that would eventually lead him to Leadville. Realizing he had some more miles to cover and upset at the world, Brian stopped in the trail and screamed out at no one and at everyone. "I Just Want To Be…Done!" His voice was coarse and dry. With an agonizing step forward, Brian lowered his head, summoned every ounce of strength, motivation and began running again.

His mental faculties were nearly unable to keep up with much more than running and breathing. Brian wanted to figure out where he was on the course, to have some idea of how much further he had to go, but his brain would not function in such detail. His mental fortitude and focus were completely exhausted. All that his rational thought and physical coordination could handle was simply putting one foot in front of the other while lifting his feet high enough off the ground so as not to trip over the smallest imperfections on the trails. Where 24 hours before, his stride was light and powerful, now it felt heavy, awkward, and foreign.

This section of trail took him away from Turquoise Lake and eventually returned to State Route 4. As mentally taxed as Brian was, it was when he saw the sign for Sugar Loafin Campgrounds that he snapped back to the present, knowing he was about three or maybe it was four miles from the finish. As much as he had loved the idea of running Leadville nearly 24 hours ago, right here, right now he hated the place. At this stage in the game all he wanted, all he could think about, was stopping. He wanted to be done. He wanted the pain in his feet to end. He wanted to sit down and he wanted to wash the layers of dirt off his face. He wanted to brush his teeth. Knowing that the end was near, Brian lowered his head, fixed his eyes on the road and concentrated on the very next step. He could think about nothing more and nothing less.

With each "next step," Brian worked his way down the road some locals called the Boulevard, one agonizing stride at a time. Mirroring the way an old steam locomotive may have entered the town in the old days, with each breath he snorted out his nostrils, "One step, just one more step," like the steam being jettisoned out of the engines stack. This rhythmic method worked as Brian pounded his way down the trail, whittling away the last painful miles.

Brian raised his eyes off the trail long enough to catch sight of Lake Country High School. This milestone he knew well. He had run past there many times in training. As his eyes grew brighter, his mind began to come alive again. He continued to hammer away at the remaining distances. With the high school in sight, he knew his goal was finally reachable. He knew that finally, this race was going to be over. He knew that soon he could finally stop running. To have this day end successfully, all he had to do was continue to press forward. He only needed to keep moving. A left turn on McWethy Drive. His legs continued to drive forward, each stride shortening the remaining distance until he would cross the finish line and this race would be over.

Reaching this landmark, Brian knew his day was just about done. It was also here that he noticed the sun begin to rise in the morning sky. A new day brought an increasing glimmer of a new life. A lump formed in his throat and breathing became even more difficult, but as hard as it was, he continued to move toward the finish. Next up was a simple right-hand turn that brought him onto 6th Street and more importantly, the finish would be within reach and within sight.

The Finish

Once on 6th Street, it was a short eight-tenths of a mile to the finish line. Brian raised his stare off the road in front of him and smiled. It was great to see Leadville again. It was great to be back within the world. Just as the relief and joy set in, so did the panic. He had no idea what time it was. His GPS watch and its backup battery had died a while back. It panicked him that the sun was in the sky, had it just risen or had it been up for hours? Brian's limited mental powers could not figure out what time of the day it was.

He reasoned with himself, "You made all the check-points. There are a lot of runners behind you, you're good, calm down and just run."

6th Street grew shorter and shorter with each foot-fall. He could hear the crowd and he could see the finish line banner. Brian's eyes scanned the crowd. He was desperate to see a familiar face. Running solo was difficult in having to care for and carry nearly all your support items. The challenge of the solo run that he had underestimated was the absence of contact with family, friends or loved ones who truly were invested in the effort. He had witnessed over and over again as runners linked up with support crews and saw the emotional uplift this provided. Brian was searching the crowd seeking his own emotional boost. Then his heart nearly burst out of his chest with what he saw next.

Off in the distance far enough so that he could not read the displayed numbers was the official timing clock. Upon seeing this Brian, strained his eyes trying to zero in, trying to get a read on the official time. Try as he might, he just could not make out the numbers that were displayed. Again he worried if he would finish in time. Did he make the 30-hour cutoff? Then, like a lightning bolt shocking whomever it came into contact with, it hit him with the equivalent of 50,000 volts. The numbers counting off from the official event time started with a two. A two was not a three, Brian reasoned, "A two must surely mean I've got time left." His heart had survived the constant workload of running nearly 100 miles. It had survived the two climbs over Hope Pass and it had survived being lost along the trail leading from Turquoise Lake. But his heart nearly exploded in joy and relief when Brian knew he would finish well within the cut off time.

Brian never stopped moving forward, but at the same time he glanced to the heavens and said, "Abby, I can't believe I made it." Calmness came across his mind and stillness entered his heart. In the middle of the road, during the finish of the hardest challenge of his life, he found peace.

From someplace a comforting thought came over him. "Brian, it's okay for you to love again. Let life and love in. And trust her."

It became hard to breathe. He had nearly finished the hardest race of his life and he had finally felt like it was okay to let go. He would never forget Abby; he knew she wanted him to move on. Squinting into the morning sun, about 100 yards from the finish his eyes spied a familiar face.

On the left side of the road, Michele stood just beyond the red carpet that would bring him to the official Leadville Trail 100 finish line. Seeing her there was nearly too much. He had been stripped raw by the mountains. This race had challenged him physically and emotionally and now his soul was exposed. He fought to hold it all together, but his eyes exploded with tears as his face became caught up and twisted with his emotions.

While captured in the excitement of seeing Michele, something else caught his eye and did what 100 miles could not do. Brian stopped dead in his tracks; he stopped running. He just stood there within sight of the red carpet and the finish.

The crowd was caught off guard. Many standing along the finish line thought something was wrong. Had he given up so close to the end? Had his heart or a vital body part failed? He stood there smiling and in tears.

Running towards him was a 14-pound ball of silver and gray fur. Her ears swept back in the wind, her tongue rolling out the right side of her mouth. Brian could hear the sound of four paws impacting the asphalt with each stride propelling her towards him. Half-hidden behind her trademark eyebrows were two wide open brown eyes that were locked on him. Brian's heart melted.

Hanna was all feet and paws, giving it everything she had to get to her daddy. The crowd that witnessed this scene let out a collective sigh. Brian did not think to question how Michele had gotten Hanna to the finish line. Even if he would have thought to ask, he didn't care.

At top speed, Hanna came roaring up to him and nearly knocked him over as she collided with the side of his calf. Brian slowly bent over and scooped her up in his arms. "Hanna-girl, man, I'm sure happy to see you…Let's finish this." Brian spoke in broken words intermixed with raw emotions. Hanna overly excited licked his dirty, sweat-stained face. She didn't care, her daddy was home. In only the way that man's best friend can do, she sensed her daddy needed her.

Brian looked back at Michele. She blew them both a kiss and signaled for him to finish. With Hanna dog in his arms, letting out a deep groan, Brian got moving again toward the finish line. A solid day of commitment and unrelenting determination was about to end. The weeks and months of untold miles, a lifetime of challenges all came together in the last ten yards. Approaching that line drawn temporally across the ground, his breathing became difficult. His mind was flooded with emotions. His legs began to get heavy. The final yards of his adventure were battling him right to the very end. This finish would see no finishers kick, no lean at the tape to beat out a competitor and no course record. Brian simply kept up a determined, slow and steady gait as he moved step by step closer to the end. Then as his last stride propelled his body across the finish line it was over. Brian journey ended with Hanna in his arms.

In simple terms, Brian had finished the Leadville Trail 100 Mile Endurance Race. Leadville is more than a race. Leadville is more than a 100 Mile race. Finishing the "Race Across The Sky" was about more than simply collecting a finisher's medal and a shiny finisher's belt buckle. On legs that were about to give out, he staggered through the race officials who were trying to offer him help. He wasn't trying to be rude or unappreciative, he was merely a man on a mission. Once across the finish line he only wanted to reach Michele and tell her everything was going to be okay.

Michele made her way to the finish line as fast as she could. Once on the other side of the finishing area, just a scant 10 feet beyond the line, she ducked under the temporary rope barriers that separated the spectators from the finishers. Once free of the obstacle, she closed the small gap between them. As she approached the man whom she knew changed her outlook on life, she reached out and held his face with her soft hands. She noticed his face was covered in dust, grit and dirt. She could tell that this race had been a battle both emotionally and physically. She could also tell that he had won. There was a sparkle in his tired eyes.

"Brian," she said. "I" taking a long deep breath, Michele continued. "I love you."

Those words released a tidal wave of emotions inside of him. They released feelings, released questions and doubts he had carried over the last 100 miles and for the years since Abby passed. He finally believed he could stop running. Hearing those three words and the emotion behind them, Brian finally felt liberated from his past. The grueling 100 miles and the crossing of Hope Pass, twice, somehow released all of the rejection, the heartbreak, disappointment and the loss that was beginning to define his life. Just as running Leadville would change his outlook on what he could accomplish physically, overcoming the mental and emotional challenge of the race provided a revitalized outlook on his life.

Michele pressed forward even closer and wrapped her arms around Brian's neck. She did not allow the sweat, trail grit or his battle worn appearance stop her. She pulled him into her tightly and they embraced as those standing around them applauded.

Hanna sandwiched between them licked their faces as she snuggled her muzzle under their chins. Lost in all of the emotions surrounding the end of the race, displaced by two souls being united was that one little dog who was so very happy to have her daddy back. Her short cropped tail wagged from side to side.

Summoning every ounce of strength he had left, Brian was able to get out two very important and perhaps life changing statements. His voiced was weak and raspy from the volume of air that he had consumed over the last 24 plus hours. Dry from the effects of the dust and cracked with emotion, it was almost painful for him to speak. "Yes, Hanna-girl, I'm very happy to be home too." Brian with his lungs heaving took a deep breath. "Michele, with one L."

He paused to look deep into her eyes taking in her deep hazel green eyes and a bright and vibrant smile, "You have shown me that I don't have to run from my past. That I still have feelings. That I'm still capable of." His voice broke off as he took another deep breath.

"You showed me that I could love again. And…"

There was a slight pause.

"I love you."

Brian finished the Leadville Trail 100 Mile Endurance Race in 26 hours, 51 minutes and 5 seconds, at just after 7 a.m. on Sunday morning.

The End

Running to Leadville

Cover Photo Provided by Jon Fredrick Photography:

Based out of Boston Massachusetts, Jon offers professional services including: Weddings, Engagements, Commercial, Events/Sports and Landscapes. Photography with an artistic flair.

In his words, everybody owns a pencil. Maybe that pencil is a Staedtler, or maybe it is just a 2-hb that we learned to draw with in High School. That pencil is a tool, and for an artist, an extension of their soul. It doesn't matter how much it costs, not everyone can make that pencil do magic. But in the hands of Leonardo da Vinci, the type of pencil doesn't matter.

The camera is my tool, an extension of my soul. It is my pencil. It is a passion, an expression of my mind. I capture moments that others might miss, and create a visual reproduction of something that may only have been a memory. Photography is art, essentially a still shot of the brain; when that shutter snaps shut, just like a blink of an eye, that moment is stored. That moment is saved, it is remembered just as it was, forever.

I'm not going to leave you holding a picture in your hand as you tell a friend, "Well if you had only of been there....." Instead, I am going to put them in that moment, to smell the ocean air, to feel the breeze as a sunset closes out the perfect day. To capture that moment is to understand the meaning of life. Because the greatest moments need to be remembered, just as they were. Beautiful, stunning, and vivid.

Visit Jon's website at:
http://jonfrederickphotography.zenfolio.com/

Running to Leadville

ABOUT THE AUTHOR:

Brian is presently a Mechanical Skills Instructor with a fortune 100 company living and working out of North Carolina and Virginia. Prior to his present position he retired from the United States Air Force after serving as a Senior Noncommissioned Officer (SMSgt). During his 20 year military career, his travels had him living in five states. Brian also served tours overseas including a remote tour to Thule, Greenland and a combat tour in Northern Iraq. Prior to his military service , he spent time as a Real Estate Agent and Sales Associate at an auto parts store in Erie, Pa.

Not a natural runner Brian found his passion for running in his 30s. Since then his running career has seen him complete race distances from 5k to 100 miles in length all across the country and overseas.

Likewise, his writing came on late. Brian could always tell a gripping story but found it hard to get it onto paper. Running To Leadville is his first novel although he has been published in national running publications, running theme blogs and his own blog at http://briansrunningadventures.com

Follow Brian on Twitter and Instagram @cledawgs or like his page on Facebook.

43271837R00113

Made in the USA
Middletown, DE
05 May 2017